Read It Again
3630 Peachtree Pkwy, Ste 314
Suwanee, GA 30024
770-232-9331
www.Read-it-Again.com

Jesús Balmori

BIRDS OF FIRE
A Filipino War Novel

Translated from the Spanish by
Robert S. Rudder
&
Ignacio López-Calvo

Dulzorada Press

BIRDS OF FIRE: A FILIPINO WAR NOVEL

Copyright © 2022, Dulzorada Press
Originally written in Spanish by Jesús Balmori between 1942-1945, and first published in 2010 as *Los Pájaros de Fuego: Novela Filipina de la Guerra* (ed. Isaac Donoso Jiménez). Instituto Cervantes - Manila.

English translation © 2022, Robert S. Rudder, Ignacio López-Calvo
Prologue © 2022, Ignacio López-Calvo

Photo captions on pp. 6, 55, 103, 149 © 2022, C. Peter Chen
Photo caption on p. 252 © 2022, David Stubblebine

Special thanks to C. Peter Chen and World War II Database (WW2DB.com) for their kind permission to use content from their website and provide us with detailed information about the sources. All images used in this volume are in the public domain.

© 2022, Dulzorada Press
Editor-in-chief: José Garay Boszeta
Email: jose@dulzorada.com
Book design and layout: Miguel Garay Boszeta
Email: miguel@dulzorada.com
Dulzorada logo design: Bidkar Yapo | @nacionchicha.pe

All rights reserved. No part of this publication may be reproduced, distributed, or transmitted in any form or by any means, including photocopying, recording, or other electronic or mechanical methods, without the prior written permission of the publisher, except in the case of brief quotations embodied in critical reviews and certain other noncommercial uses permitted by copyright law.

Library of Congress Control Number: 2021953493

ISBN: 978-1-953377-10-4 (paperback)
ISBN: 978-1-953377-11-1 (hardcover)
Published by Dulzorada Press
http://Dulzorada.com

Printed in the USA

(Previous page) Manila, Philippines during Japanese occupation, 9 May 1942.
Source: Japanese Army
Retrieved from: https://ww2db.com/image.php?image_id=4259

CONTENTS

Prologue   9
by Ignacio López-Calvo

BIRDS OF FIRE: A FILIPINO WAR NOVEL

    Part I   61

    Part II   105

    Part III   151

    Part IV   201

Prologue[*]
Ignacio López-Calvo

If, according to Jorge Mojarro, Jesús Balmori (1886-1948; a.k.a. Batikuling) inaugurates literary Modernismo in the Philippines with his 1904 poetry collection Rimas malayas (Malay Rhymes) (Mojarro, 2019 "Teodoro" 234), he also tries to put an end to its influence in his posthumous novel *Los pájaros de fuego* (Firebirds, 2010). However, Miguel Ángel Feria points out that one can find Modernista poems in Filipino newspapers as early as the end of the nineteenth century (247). Feria adds that one can notice Modernista influences, soon after the publication of Balmori's *Rimas Malayas*, in José Palma's *Melancólicas* (Melancholic, 1912) and Fernando María Guerrero's *Crisálidas*... (Chrysalis..., 1914), but also later works, such as Cecilio Apóstol's *Pentélicas*, published posthumously in 1950, or Guerrero's posthumous *Aves y flores* (Birds and Flowers, 1971) (Feria 249). According to Mojarro, these influences are also present in Hilario Zialcita y Legarda's poetry collection *La Nao de Manila* (The Manila Galleon, 1913).[1]

Indeed, Latin American Modernismo influenced Spanish-language Filipino writers, and Balmori in particular, but this influence came to an abrupt end. The limits of literary Modernismo are apparent in *Los pájaros de fuego*, a novel that openly rejects the Japonaiserie

---

[*] I am indebted to Jorge Mojarro for his feedback on this prologue and, in particular, for pointing out the protracted influence of Modernismo in Apóstol's and Zialcita's writing.

popularized by Latin American modernistas, including the Nicaraguan Rubén Darío, whom Balmori deeply admired. It also closes the door on the Orientalist affinities of modernistas as a direct result of the advent of the Pacific War and the brutal Japanese occupation of the Philippines (1942-1945).[2] Balmori, who had previously declared his profound admiration for Japanese culture and civilization in his literature and speeches, eventually ran into the wall of reality upon observing the unspeakable brutality of the Japanese occupation of the Philippines.

As Beatriz Álvarez-Tardío, Beatriz Barrera, Reynaldo D. Coronel Jr., Isaac Donoso, Miguel Ángel Feria, Jorge Mojarro, and other critics have demonstrated, the influence of Latin American Modernismo on Spanish-language Filipino literature is unquestionable. It is a case of peripheral, South-South cross-cultural exchange, even though it may very well have taken place via Spain, which at the time was still casting a hegemonic cultural shadow over its former colonies. Just like Filipino writers had previously been trying to catch up with European Romanticism (Balmori, for example, never hides his admiration for Gustavo Adolfo Bécquer), they saw the influence of Rubén Darío, José Martí, and other modernistas as a way to update their own emerging Spanish-language literary tradition.[3] In fact, (self-) Orientalization and Japonism in Filipino letters was, in part, evidence of the influence of Latin American Modernismo. Yet, it eventually took a different turn from the original escapism and exoticism sought out by Latin American modernistas acquiring instead nationalist overtones, as Donoso has pointed out; after all, not only were Filipino writers a real-life part of this so-called mysterious "Orient" imagined by Darío and his followers, but some, like Balmori, also had personal experience and knowledge of countries like Japan.

Jesús Balmori, on the left.
(Excelsior Magazine. Gus Vibal Private Collection. Courtesy of Jorge Mojarro)

Born in Manila, Balmori began to read his poetry in public at the age of fifteen. Two years later, he published *Rimas malayas* (Malay Rhymes, 1904), the first modernista Filipino text. Initially inspired by Spanish Romantic poets such as José de Espronceda and Bécquer, he was later even more impressed with Darío's Modernista poetry. The emulation of the Nicaraguan's style and vocabulary is noticeable, for instance, in the second section of his poem "Tríptico real" (Royal Triptych), titled "Victoria de Battemberg:"

> Strawberry and snow and velvet woman
> As smooth as breeze kisses
> In whose eyes the blue of the sky
> Is a flower of light broken in smiles;
> Fairy asleep in pale and resounding
> Ideal dream of love and discretion,
> Whose fragrant gold hair
> Scented a king among its threads;
> Gentle queen of aroma and wonders
> Whom a people kneeling
> As the custody of its faith venerates.
> Not from Isabel the splendorous blood
> Runs in your veins. But you are a rose
> That has Spain open in its flag! (My translation)[4]

The poem's exuberant chromatism ("Strawberry and snow and velvet woman;" "the blue of the sky") and its references to precious minerals and stones ("fragrant gold hair") are reminiscent of French Parnassians' influences in Latin American Modernista writing. Likewise, the appeal to human senses like that of smell ("scented a king among its threads;" "Gentle queen of aroma and wonders;" "you are a rose"); the vocabulary ("Fairy," "ideal"); and the musicality typical of the influence of French symbolism ("los besos de las brisas" ["the breeze kisses"]), all evoke modernista aesthetics.

At other times Balmori finds inspiration in Darío's lyrical lines, such as the famous "There are a thousand cubs loosed from the Spanish lion"[5] in his poem "A Roosevelt" ("To Roosevelt"), which is echoed in Balmori's lines "Old and noble Castilian Lioness . . . the cubs rumble,"[6] included in his poem "Canto a España" (Song to Spain). Similarly, the rhythm, tone, topics, and vocabulary of his "Ingratitud" (Ingratitude) is redolent of Darío's "Sonatina," included in *Prosas profanas y otros poemas* (*Profane Hymns and Other Poems*, 1896):

I

Sitting on a throne
Made of pearls and roses
A thousand beautiful fairies
Preluding songs made her sleep,
Silent the night;
The moonlight
Plated one by one
The giant towers of the gentile palace.

II

Below, the poet
Moaning a lament,
The wind was taking
Far away his love echoes

The girl listened
The loving lament,
Her pink lips
Murmured telling to the fairies: Sorry!

III

The fairies did not hear
His sad prayer;
Mute and lonely
The slender sleeping princess stayed,
And the poet trembling,
Confused and gloomy
Felt so cold
That the golden lyre in the mud threw.

IV

How indecisive this story
You barely understand?
I know you understand
The legend that sad forged my illusion,
Your love is the group
Of fairies, restless;
My soul the poet,
The slender princess my unhappy heart.

Tellingly, copying part of the first line of Darío's "Sonatina," Balmori published a dramatic short story titled "La princesa está triste" (The Princess Is Sad), in *Revista Filipina / The Philippine Review* in March 1919).

Photo of the publication of Jesús Balmori's short story "La princesa está triste" (The Princess Is Sad), in Revista Filipina / The Philippine Review in March 1919)

As for Balmori's Orientalist tendencies, we find a prime example in his "La gueisha" (The Geisha), included in the collection *Mi casa de Nipa* (My House in Nipa, 1941):

It's night, it's a hall, and it's eleven.
A gong sounds like an old bronze violin.
A gold and burgundy curtain is drawn,
And in the scene that simulates a new Orient
Advances quietly, slowly,
The enameled porcelain doll.

One would think of a great aroma of mignonettes
All wrapped in her golds and her silks
Under a musical rhythm that goes up and up.
It is a bird? Is it a flower? It is not flower or bird,
It's the languorous, sweet, soft geisha,
Like the trembling passage of a cloud.

She is going to dance. It is a mysterious dance,
It's a flight, it's the rose bud
That in the lantern light becomes a flower.
One can't see her feet under her finery.
She only moves her two hands, white wings,
White oars of a dream about rowing.

Under the triumph of the rhyming music,
The entire dance is a grave pantomime,
And the geisha, sovereign sunflower,
To the sounds of the flutes, smiling,
rises in snake-like spirals,
Or bends like a lotus under the sun.

What is she telling us with her solemn movements?
What are her small, slow steps telling us?
What oriental story is this one in the dance
That while opening the crescent of her eyes
One would think her hope is pierced
With thistles like a poor butterfly?

Is it sadness? Is it joy that she feels?
What scented mystery of the East,
What divine, magical, religious rite
Unwraps as in the waves of an aroma
This flower, this woman, this dove,
With the rhythm of her graceful body?

The tan-tan will tell you. Her fiancé,
The one who knows about her kisses, has left
And the poor geisha does not know where he is;
He left in search of glory and fortune
In the night without stars and without moon;
      Will he return? Will he not return?

She asks shivering stars.
breezes, cedars, flowers,
The lace that breaks over the sea;
And since no one knows where her beloved went,
This geisha of the unfortunate love,
      What will she do but crying?

She asks the hurricane of broken clouds,
auras, pale seagulls,
hills of emerald and sapphire;
And since no one knows anything about her beloved,
This geisha of the sore love,
        What will she do but die?

Yes. The flutes and the geisha are dying
They are sighs and they are pearls that, falling,
Form sounds, form divine tears,
While the sound of the gong resonates again,
The rose and gold vision dissipates.
And the curtains close slowly.[7]

Balmori, as Donoso indicates, had already praised the virtues of Japanese women in his 1932 speech in verse "Nippón," and particularly in its section "Madame Crisantemo." In "La geisha," we find the usual Modernista vocabulary ("divine" [128]) as well as references to precious stones and metals or other luxury items, such as bronze, gold, silk, emerald, sapphire, and pearls. From the very title—focusing on an image of Japanese women fetishized for decades by Western travelers and writers—, the poetic voice displays a seemingly Western male gaze at an objectivized and exoticized Asian woman: "The enameled porcelain doll" (127); "It is a bird? Is it a flower? It is not flower or bird, / It's the languorous, sweet, soft geisha" (127). We then hear a stereotypical gong sound (129) and are invited to imagine "a new Orient" as an inscrutable space full of mystery: "What scented mystery of the East" (128) and "It is a mysterious dance" (128). But it is the passive, smiling geisha that elicits the biggest aura of mystery: her solemn movements, her slow, her small steps inspire this sort of Westernized voyeur-poet. Balmori's geisha is sad, like Darío's princess in "La sonatina," and wonders about the whereabouts of her beloved (he left in search of glory and fortune) and whether he will ever return. Eventually, in a melodramatic and romantic image, the suffering Japanese woman, an example of faithfulness to her husband, has no alternative but to die of love. All in all, the geisha, as representative of the Japanese woman, is the ideal loyal and subservient wife imagined by the fantasizing poet. Simultaneously, she embodies all the refinement and sophistication of Japanese culture (as will be seen, this view will be somewhat contradicted at the end of his novel *Los pájaros de fuego*).

Geishas continue to be a source of inspiration in Balmori's poem "El cuento de la Geisha" (The Geisha's Story), written in Tokyo in May 1912, according to the author:[8]

> A rare music of flutes and cymbals,
> Rumbles under the metallic noise of a gong;
> A curtain of birds and yellow suns rises
> And under a huge wave of polychromatic shinning
> She arises in a slow, gentle genuflection.
>
> She is pale. Her flesh of unknown nacres
> Or was perhaps made of gold of the moon;
> One would think it fell from reveries
> Because her body is a glass of scented lotuses
> And her badly shod feet are like two pearls.

She advances. All her lines and fineries triumph
In diaphanous glories of rhinestones and tulle,
And while the applause is heard through the rooms
Her arms rise slowly, as if they were wings
And silks of purple and blue are flying.

She will tell us a story, you will see; one of those stories
That someone told her in her paternal home
While blossoms woke up in the cherry trees,
When she still did not know about kisses
Or about another divine thing, loving.

She will tell us about it, singing. Listen. Pause. Another pause
The rose of her mouth begins:

The Mandarin
Old and libidinous and ugly, was the cause
For the pretty girl from Nishitausa Island

To shade her jasmine leaves with mud.
The crazy grandfather gave her away in exchange for some gold
To calm his burning thirst with sake,
While she drank the wine of her weeping
And the Mandarin loved her while drooling on her: I adore you!
Oh little goldfish that captivated my thirst!
Oh, what disgust for gems, golds, and flowers,
The roses and ties of his royal pagoda.
How scary his eyes of lyrical glares!
What horror the warm chamber of incense in shinning

Where is an altar of silk and coral bed?
On a night full of stars, the captive
Loaded the old Mandarin's pipe with opium,
And fled without even knowing where she was going.
She ran away from that flame where they were throwing her alive
And got lost in the floating shadows of the garden.
And she was never found. Never her uncertain step
Guided her unknown route, her tremulous passing,
That, in vain, they believed to be a broken flower in the orchard
And in vain, on suspicion that she had died
They beat the loud foams of the sea.
What happened to the girl from Nishitausa Island?...
(His voice in the question trembles. The gong is crying)
What happened because of the Mandarin's girl?
What happened to the girl?...
(There is a long pause.
The gong keeps crying).
She, meanwhile, leaves.

She leaves. All their lines and fineries have trembled
Like a lotus that a kiss got confused,
And while the applause is heard through the rooms
Her hands rise slowly as if they were waves
And kisses fly under the shaking of the gong![9]

Following the poem's last line, Balmori makes it clear that he wrote it while in Tokyo, perhaps for the verisimilitude or authenticity effect. However, he seems to confuse Japanese topics with typically Chinese ones, such as opium consumption and Mandarins. This poem, like the previous one, displays the usual modernista vocabulary ("A rare music") and Parnassian overtones in its appeal to human senses: multiple colors—especially blue—and sounds; smells of cherry flowers, lotuses, roses, and jasmines; precious metals, stones and coveted fabrics (gold, gems, pearls, rhinestones, coral, tulle, silk). And coinciding with "La geisha," Balmori refers to worn-out Orientalist clichés, like the gong.

The geisha is again objectified and exoticized by being described as having a pale complexion, slow movements, and a mysterious nature: "Her flesh of unknown nacres" (234). The poetic voice describes her almost immaterial nature as having fallen off a dream and then fetishizes her feet as pearls and her arms as wings. Unlike the passive object of desire in "La geisha," the Japanese woman in "El cuento de la Geisha" has more agency, as she sings the story of a young virgin who is sold by her alcoholic grandfather. The man who purchases her denotes another Orientalist motif: an old, ugly, lascivious, drooling mandarin in a room full of incense and horror: "How scary his eyes of lyrical glares!" (235). Eventually, the sad and scared young woman manages to escape by adding a large dose of opium to the old man's pipe and fleeing once he falls asleep. As seen, both of these poems resort to Orientalist and modernista aesthetics to evoke a world of mystery and exotic sensuality that is more enticing to Western males than to Asians.

For many years, Balmori was considered an accomplished poet. However, his first published novels, *Bancarrota de almas* ["Bankruptcy of Souls"] (1911) and *Se deshojó la flor* ["The Flower's Petals Have Fallen"] (1915), would change the perception that he was only a poet. These novels remain, for the most part, exempt from national and international politics, though the former includes a heated dialogue about the pros and cons of Filipino political independence. Both instead harshly criticize the nation's bourgeois conservative morals and the hypocrisy of the Catholic Church.

The plot of *Bancarrota de almas* is quite simple: it describes a love triangle between the seventeen-year-old Ángela Limo, her cousin and boyfriend Ventura, and a smooth-talking poet, Augusto Valdivia (Balmori). After defeating Ventura in fisticuffs, Augusto wins Ángela's heart and leaves her with child before suddenly succumbing to tuberculosis. She then marries Ventura who is unaware of her condition; after the wedding, she informs him of her pregnancy. In the following passage, we find a sharp criticism of traditional social mores through Augusto's justification for becoming inebriated and visiting brothels:

> A man gets drunk, as I have done, to ease the pain of his dire poverty, of his weaknesses, of being cowardly unable to withstand life's blows outright; a man goes to buy an hour of love when he has no one in the world who loves him, when he is alone and terrified by his loneliness, when he is so hungry and thirsty for a kiss that he does not care whether the mouth that is about to kiss him is that of a saint or devil. This is not understood by those who have full stomachs, those self-righteous ones who go around pompously shouting "Morals!... Pooh to morals! I know much about these big shots, things that, if published, would even disgust dogs.[10]

Augusto, defending Epicurean philosophy, assures Ángela that there is "nothing dirtier, nothing more ridiculous that the morals of men."[11] He insists that many women who claim to be saints are, in reality,

Messalina (Emperor Claudius's promiscuous wife), and many self-righteous men are, deep inside, depraved.

Balmori also resorts to eroticism to *épater les bourgeois*: "They were arguing over the shower. Margarita's shirt slightly opened revealing a round, erect breast resembling a billiard ball, tanned under its red nipple, like a strawberry. Angela placed her hand over it, squeezing it; she jumped, unable to open her eyes filled with soap foam."[12] Likewise, perhaps, the author includes in these novels anticlerical passages that reveal the excessive puritanism and hypocrisy of the Catholic clergy and his negative views on the institution of marriage: "Speaking ill of the Jesuits, he engaged his aunt in a heated discussion. 'They are lazy, believe me, hypocrites; up to now, all they do is cause all the damage they can,'"[13] Ventura argues. And later, "Were there no donkeys?" "No ma'am, friars only date back to the middle ages only."[14] And neither does the author make any attempt to hide his modernista influences: "Ventura, under an electric lamp, was casually reading Darío's 'Azul'; its charming verses seemed passionate, passionate like Angela's kisses."[15] A few pages later the narrator describes Augusto reading the poetry collection *Alma América* by the Peruvian Modernista José Santos Chocano.

In his second novel, *Se deshojó la flor. Novela filipina* (1915), Balmori distances himself even more from political matters. As in his first novel, he resorts to the same romantic and modernista aesthetics, with a Modernista vocabulary (numerous references to silk and precious stones) and an erotic-filled tone: "And Rafael, finding himself before a modest, sweetly breathless Leonarda, wondered if what had happened in that room was all a dream, whether it was he who caressed and kissed the godly body of that lovely girl."[16] Sporadic, anticlerical attacks reappear in this novel as well.

The plot describes the immoral and melodramatic adventures of an older Don Juan-type, Rafael Lozano, who decides to ignore what he considers Filipino puritanical morals. Married to a woman named Dolores, with whom he cannot have children, he has an affair with her sister, Leonarda, who has a boyfriend named Crisóstomo Cristóbal. Characters become jealous of each other throughout to such an extreme that Rafael's wife, Dolores, aware of her husband's many infidelities, dies of a broken heart. But this is what, for some time, Rafael had been hoping, so that he could then marry Leonarda. Later, after Rafael falls in love with a younger woman, Rosario "Charing" Silva ("Charing," her nickname, is based on the name Charo, which is how women named Rosario are often called), he suddenly begins to bemoan Dolores's death and to recognize that she was his only true love. The widower searches for solace in the company of his sisters who live in the countryside but, of course, he once again falls in love with yet another young woman who lives there, Margarita, for no other reason than that she reminds him of Dolores. Meanwhile, Leonarda invites him to her wedding and, before the ceremony, the suffering widower blackmails her into having sex with him for the last time or he will publicly reveal the location of one of her moles. In yet another inconsistent plot twist, Leonarda suddenly starts to miss him as he is walking out the door. He, on the other hand, while in this shaky love affair, begins to so miss his late wife that he commits suicide, as any good romantic protagonist would do.

Balmori's third and last novel, *Pájaros de fuego*, is quite different from the others in that Modernista aesthetics are predominant at the plot's beginning only to disappear once the harsh reality of World War II sets in. Initially an avowed admirer of all things Japanese, Balmori visited Yokohama in 1902, at the age of sixteen, and later participated in the dissemination of the Meiji political propaganda. Thus, in his 1932 poetic address "Nippón," delivered at the headquarters of the Japanese Association of the Philippines, Balmori praises Japanese civilization, its achievements, and even acknowledges the divine origins of the Japanese emperor. According to Donoso this "constitutes the recognition by a Filipino citizen of the superiority of Japan's emperors and, consequently, of the power of the Japanese Empire in Asia."[17]

In this novel, perhaps his best, Don Lino Robles, Balmori's alter ego and protagonist, reiterates the same belief in imperial divinity as he explains:

> All Japanese gods are included in the strange mythology of the Empire, its golden legend, its first milestone in assuming the throne. Because Izanami, passionate and in love, continued to give birth after her great geographical birth. Eventually, Amaterasu, goddess of the sun, emerged, along with her brother Susanoo, god of courage, who married her. It is from those delirious nights of passion that the Emperors of Japan descend.[18]

A few pages later, Don Lino vehemently insists: "Japan was the spirit of gods who embodied 'shoguns,' 'samurai' and 'daimios'. Why did they not allow it to move forward without a white power impeding its course?"[19] Having lived in Japan for three years, the protagonist seems to have bought into the imperial concept of a Greater East Asia Co-Prosperity Sphere, promulgated by Foreign Minister Hachirō Arita on 29 June 1940. This aspiration included an alleged Asian cultural and economic unity under the understood leadership of the Empire of

Japan that would be self-sufficient and free from Western imperialist domination. However, the notion of the Greater East Asia Co-Prosperity Sphere was a pretext for Japanese imperial control and manipulation over eventually occupied countries. The idea was to benefit the Empire's economy through its military might and extractivism.

Don Lino, in arguments with his brother Don Ramón, firmly supports Japan's right to be the sovereign leader of the new Pacific Asia:

> The Japanese are a people who love children, flowers, deer, water, and birds; who hold honor as the only and true religion, and believe their homeland to be the only and true altar; who do not mind sacrificing their lives and finances for the survival and glory of the empire whose calling is, by its extraordinary strength and indomitable spirit, to reign over the Pacific, the master of the East, the ruler of the new Asia....[20]

He even justifies China's brutal occupation by the Japanese: "China must be treated thus! China is being civilized, as it deserves and wants, with bullets."[21] From the onset of the narrative, Don Lino fails to see the ominous signs of an imminent occupation when Kenjiro, one of his two Japanese gardeners (imperial spies), foreshadowing the tragedy, declares: "There is no Japanese who does not see it (the Philippines) as his own land. What difference does it make? A day will come, sir, when the entire East, all of Asia, will become one people, one great Empire..."[22]

Before *Los pájaros de fuego*, Balmori seemed to be content, in certain writings, with his nation being viewed by the Japanese government as its backyard, as a land in need of the paternal guidance of a more economically and technologically advanced Asian nation like Japan. After all, in his view, Japan was also an Asian country, unlike the previous and current colonial powers in the Philippines, Spain and the United States. Initially, to this proud Nipponophile, the prosperous Land of the Rising Sun represents "the principal nation of the world"[23] and, as such, a model for other Asian countries to emulate. Balmori and his semiautobiographical protagonist's veneration of Japanese culture and political leadership, however, will come to a halt with the ensuing invasion of the islands and the destruction of Manila, with its entire (material and immaterial) Spanish colonial heritage.

This drastic change of mind is—despite the subtitle of the novel, *Novela filipina de la guerra* ["Filipino War Novel"]—the true leitmotif of a novel that Balmori wrote mostly during the Japanese occupation, with its fourth part handwritten a few months after the end of the World War II, as the author explains in his foreword. Whereas the first chapters introduce a Filipino protagonist still impassioned with Japanese culture and society, the ultra-violent invasion of his country leaves him no alternative but to admit his misconceptions about Japanese chivalry, genteelness, and kindness. At one point, Japanese imperial soldiers take over his house, steal all they find, including his cars, rape his housemaids, rape and murder his pregnant daughter, and abuse him physically. As a result, Don Lino loses his mind and dies alone, in utter sorrow and regret, at a riverbed in one of his haciendas.

Along the way, the novel, now devoid of *modernista* influence, portrays, from a polyphonic perspective, the growing seed of Filipino nationalism in the face of Japanese oppression. On the one hand, Don Lino nostalgically expresses his gratitude to the previous Spanish colonialists and, though he is not very fond of the United States, he opposes their intention of giving the Philippines its independence:

> Don Lino, like several Filipino rich men, did not like Americans, nor was he satisfied with their desire to grant the country independence.... Independence would ruin Filipinos. Only four empowered puppets who could benefit from it would want it. The people would not benefit from it. They were not, nor would they be for a long time, ready to take on such a great responsibility.[24]

By contrast, his son Fernando, who has become a guerilla captain in charge of more than one thousand men fighting the Japanese, rejects all types of colonialism, both Spanish and American. Somehow, it seems as if the old Nipponophile protagonist and the new, awakened protagonist along with his militant son Fernando were the three stages of Balmori's lifelong political development. Fernando (the last stage) represents a decolonial view of Filipino identity, ready for any type of sacrifice to achieve political and intellectual independence from all foreigners. Thus, he is reminiscent of Lapu-Lapu, who fought against the Spanish invaders, and José Rizal, the father of Filipino independence:

> And as powerful as they were [Spanish colonizers], pretending that their gold chains were garlands of flowers, they tied our hands. Gold chains but, nonetheless chains! Then we lost the best thing that God had given us, our freedom! And ever since then, we await day and night for the right moment to unfasten our shackles. That is why the poet fell, singing as he faced death and Bonifacio loudly proclaimed our independence.[25]

Eventually, however, Fernando Robles ends up wounded, mistreated, and emaciated in a Japanese concentration camp, as did many other Filipino officers.

In turn, his uncle Don Ramón is the most politically astute character; he constantly mocks his brother's Nipponophilia and warns him, to no avail, about the impending Japanese danger. In his dialogues, readers can more easily notice the end of a Romantic or Modernista approach to fiction. For instance, at one point he tells his nephew Fernando: "Hey, Fernando, is that you? May God and the Philippines bless you! And when you find yourself in front of them, don't forgive even one, kill as many as you can! Mercy was not made for them! God did not give us a heart to waste on those animals... !"[26] This language is a far cry from that in *Se deshojó la flor*!

Overall, *Los pájaros de fuego* is a key work, not because it is one of the last Spanish-language Filipino novels and the only one to relate the Japanese invasion in Spanish, but because, perhaps unconsciously, it depicts the evolution and maturity of an original and defiant nationalist thought that is turning Filipino national identity into a resistance weapon against invaders.[27] While Balmori's novel denotes literature's power to convey the collective cry of a people undergoing an unspeakable genocide, it also presages the end of Spanish-language Filipino writing and the Spanish cultural heritage in the archipelago. It reveals the misperceptions and disillusionments of a rapidly disappearing social class.

In addition, *Los pájaros de fuego* marks the end of modernista, Orientalist, and Japonist influences on Filipino writing—as stated, the influence of an aestheticizing and (self-)exoticizing Modernismo yields to a new realist, politically committed literature. In fact, the graphic horror portrayed in the fourth part of *Los pájaros de fuego* is closer to the Spanish Tremendismo of the 1940s[28] (even though he never read these authors) than to Modernismo in its harsher language and crude descriptions of Japanese atrocities in the Philippines. The old-fashioned, overly romantic, and at times sappy (from today's perspective) language of Balmori's first novels and in the initial chapters of *Los pájaros de fuego* is now gone, as the sarcastic tone of the following passage shows: "Then, they row called the housemaids and every Japanese soldier took one into a room. Through the stylish bedrooms, the wails of the maids being raped resounded, mixed with the shattering noise of glasses and bottles along with the soldiers' shouted comments and laughter as they carried out their evil deeds. Banzai Nippon;"[29] further on, "with all sorts of citizens being savagely tortured and then shot under the slightest pretext."[30] Romantic or Modernista influence has all but disappeared; instead, these horrifying scenes brings this work closer to European Naturalism:

> Allies? Men from the same race? Never! Filipinos did not descend from Asian pirates. They did not have as their ancestors wild warriors with slave women who hypocritically worshipped the shadows of the dead, death's image. The blood that ran through our veins was not yellow, like pus and bile, but red, red human blood a people's blood, God's blood.[31]

Its closing pages relate the massacres and rapes carried out by blood-thirsty Japanese soldiers as they retreated from the islands: "And Fernando, horrified, could see, before closing the balcony's doors, how a pitiful woman, falling to her knees before a Japanese soldier, held up her baby son and begged for mercy. The soldier impaled the boy with his bayonet, threw his body against the rocks, then shot the unfortunate woman."[32] These passages reveal the author's and the protagonist's rejection of their initial Nipponophilia.

Therefore, as was the case for the *tremendistas* in post-civil war Spain, whose writing reflected their personal involvement in the conflict, Balmori's tragic experience during the Japanese invasion (he lost all his possessions in the bombings) no longer allowed him to embellish his writing with self-exoticizing Orientalism. Once and for all, reality had replaced literary influence. As Donoso points out, Modernismo had been a useful tool in the articulation of a Filipino national(ist) identity: "in the case of the Philippines, the aesthetics of Modernism will be the fundamental vehicle in the creation of its own aesthetics, one that contains a political ideology based on the idea of nation building."[33] This at times included the creation of an Orientalism from the East, to which even Rizal resorted.[34] But now, a new language and tone needed to be deployed to denounce the archipelago's tragic circumstances; the harsh reality of the nation now demanded new tools for denunciation.

Donoso points out how Modernismo led to a literary idealization: "Precisely for reasons of political commitment and search for a national identity, Modernismo in the Philippines will acquire its own personality, one that will result in the idealization of the Philippines."[35] Eventually, however, Balmori will reverse this move in which he himself had participated by resorting, in *Los pájaros de fuego*, to a harsh (self-) criticism of the Filipino upper classes, together with the shameless collaboration of some sectors of Filipino society with the Japanese invaders. With its subtitle, A *Filipino War Novel*, *Los pájaros de fuego* underscores its author's patriotism, perhaps in a desperate attempt to fend off accusations of collaborationism, given his former praise of Japanese achievements. But Filipinoness is no longer idealized in pursuit of a nationalist ideology; it is now time to look in the mirror and explore what exactly went wrong with people like himself who were deceived by Japanese culture and political propaganda only to realize too late their mistake. In *Los pájaros de fuego*'s conclusion, all that Don Lino believed about Japan is belied. Even his vehement praise of Japanese women's loyalty to their partners is contradicted once his beloved Japanese lover and muse, Haruko, writes to tell him that she is pregnant and about to marry another man.

Even though Balmori visited Japan and experienced first-hand Japanese culture and society, it would not be wrong to assume that he was also influenced by the then trendy chinoiseries and Japanism of European writers and imitated by their Latin American peers. In this regard, the novel's message openly recognizes that there is no point in imitating the imported Orientalist worldviews of European and Latin American writers who admired Asian cultures, like that of the Japanese, with their personal lack of knowledge about them. Such imitation became even more ludicrous as, in the real-life "Orient," Filipinos were suffering the atrocities of the Japanese who, in turn, were following the cruel and unhinged model of European colonialism.[36]

In sum, *Los pájaros de fuego* portrays the downfall of a wealthy and distinguished family in Manila, the Robles, after the advent of the Japanese invasion. In his avowed Nipponophilia, Don Lino Robles, the head of the family, seems to be the Orientalist Balmori's alter ego. Conceiving of the Japanese Empire as a liberator of the European colonies in Asia and as a cultural referent, he mocks, particularly in the first part of the novel, his brother Don Ramón about his warning of an impending Japanese military attack. The latter is a key character in the polyphonic nature of the novel because only he dares to contradict the protagonist's obsession: not only is he convinced that Japan will invade the Philippines, but he also denies the divine origins of the emperor, decries geisha prostitution with foreigners, is shocked by humans pulling carts and by seppuku ritual suicide, and that many join the imperial army to massacre citizens of weaker nations. By the time that Don Lino finally witnesses the realization of some of his brother's fears, it is too late: his pregnant daughter Natalia is raped and killed by those Japanese soldiers who were supposed to be liberating the islands from Western imperialism. As if that were not bad enough, Don Lino must now see his own son-in-law, Sandoval, become a shameless collaborator of the Japanese.

In this national allegory, each character metonymically represents a larger societal group or a nation. Natalia Robles, the Philippine *dalaga* (unmarried woman) raped by Japanese soldiers, embodies the Philippines usurped by an immoral invader. The character Sandoval, who only marries Natalia because of her family's wealth and social position, personifies the dark side of a decadent Filipino society, a self-criticism that goes along with the open condemnation of Japanese imperialism in the Philippines. In turn, the hypocritical character of Andrade serves the same purpose: he is another social climber who, aware of the national psychology of the Filipino, cynically uses his newspaper to fawn over all those in power. During the Japanese occupation, Andrade will turn his newspaper, *La linterna*, into a servile, Japanese propaganda rag and he even tries to adopt Japanese manners and customs, like the sycophant that he is. But Andrade is not the only traitor; Don Lino bemoans how many Filipino intellectuals, moved by hunger, have become subservient collaborators of the Japanese and how many Filipinas now view themselves as geishas.

In turn, Don Lino Robles, a colonized mind that keeps thanking the two countries that colonized the archipelago, Spain and the United States, represents the affluent, but blind and self-absorbed, Filipino oligarchy that has failed to prevent the destruction of the country:

> Spain could not ignore our fate.... [It] merged us, after three centuries, with a civilization that it imported from their America, turning us into a people like no other in the East, thereby creating a race of strong, fit, worthy men. Spain laid the formidable groundwork of our national structure and the United States later capped that structure with modern pomp and practical ornaments. The Philippines owed both nations its proud past and its victorious present.[37]

Therefore, Don Lino seems to contradict himself by celebrating Japanese war advances and claiming not to trust white men because they are crazy bullies who even kill each other for insignificant reasons; all the while, he is grateful to Western colonizers and feels protected by the American presence in the Philippines. Incidentally, according to Donoso, many in the Filipino intelligentsia then supported Japanese imperialism to offset U.S. colonialism in the region.

His son, Fernando, who before the war had been in charge of one of his father's haciendas in Luzon, is still not entirely devoid of the snares of a colonized mind, as he surprisingly claims that the Philippines is free under U.S. occupation: "No, the Japanese did not come to give us our freedom, of which we had plenty, or to bring us anything other than hunger, destruction, and death."[38] Similarly, Fernando later tells a Japanese soldier, whom he holds captive, that the

Kagahastian, Raymundo. *Idealismo o patriotismo*. Nueva Era Press, 1950.

Labrador, Juan. *A Diary of the Japanese Occupation*. Santo Tomas University Press, 1989.

López de Olaguer, Antonio. *El terror amarillo en Filipinas*. Juventud, 1947.

López-Calvo, Ignacio. "From Self-Orientalization to Revolutionary Patriotism: Paterno's Subversive Discourse hidden in Romances." *Transpacific Connections of Philippine Literature in Spanish*. UNITAS, vol. 92 no. 1, May 2019, pp. 143-66.

Martín de la Cámara, Eduardo. *Parnaso filipino. Antología de poetas del archipiélago magellánico*. Hardpress, 2016.

Mojarro, Jorge. "Prólogo. Teodoro Kalaw o el curioso observador burgués." *Hacia la tierra del Zar*, Teodoro M. Kalaw, edited by Jorge Mojarro, Renacimiento, 2014.

—. "Teodoro Kalaw lee a Gómez Carrillo: *Hacia la tierra del Zar* (1908), un ejemplo de crónica modernista filipina." *Transpacific Connections of Philippine Literature in Spanish*. UNITAS, vol. 92 no. 1, May 2019, pp. 229-55.

Ortuño Casanova, Rocío. "Los sonidos de la II Guerra Mundial en Manila: ruido y autorrepresentación en *Nuestros cinco últimos días bajo el yugo nipón*, de María Paz Zamora-Mascuñana." *Revista de Crítica Literaria Latinoamericana*, edited by Jorge Mojarro, vol. XLIV, no 88, 2018, pp. 291-314.

Palma, José. *Melancólicas*. Librería Manila Filatélica, 1912.

Reyes, José G. *Terrorismo y redención. Casos concretos de atrocidades cometidas por los japoneses en Filipinas*. Cacho Hermanos, 1947.

Roa, Alfredo. *De aquella tragedia: episodios de la última guerra en Filipinas* (1947); José María Cuenco's *Memorias de un refugiado*. A.T. O, 1947.

Zamora Mascuñana, María Paz. "Nuestros cinco últimos días bajo el yugo nipón." *Cuentos cortos 1919-1923 y recuerdos de la Liberación 1945*. n.p. 1960.

Zialcita y Legarda, Hilario. *La Nao de Manila*. Caridad Sevilla, [1913] 2004.

III

Las hadas no oían
Su triste plegaria;
Muda y solitaria
La esbelta princesa dormida quedó,
Y el vate temblando,
Confuso y sombrío
Sintió tanto frío
Que la lira de oro entre el fango arrojó.

IV

¿Qué indecisa esta historia
Apenas entiendes?
Yo sé que comprendes
La leyenda que triste forjó mi ilusión,
Tu amor es la ronda
De hadas, inquieta;
Mi alma el poeta,
La esbelta princesa mi infeliz corazón.
Es de noche, es un salón, y son las once.
Suena un gong como un violón de viejo bronce.
Se descorre una cortina de oro y grana,
Y en la escena que simula un nuevo Oriente
Se adelanta quedamente, lentamente,
La muñeca de esmaltada porcelana.
Se dijera un gran aroma de resedas
Toda envuelta entre sus oros y sus sedas
Bajo un ritmo musical que sube y sube.
¿Es un ave? ¿Es una flor? No es flor ni es ave,
Es la gueisha langorosa, dulce, suave,
Como el paso tembloroso de una nube.

Va a bailar. Es una danza misteriosa,
Es un vuelo, es el capullo de una rosa
Que a la luz de los faroles se hace flor.
No se pueden ver sus pies bajo sus galas.
Sólo mueve sus dos manos, mancas alas,
Blancos remos de un ensueño bogador.

Bajo el triunfo de la música que rima,
Todo el baile es una grave pantomima,
Y la gueisha, soberana y tornasol,
A los sones de las flautas, sonriente,
Se levanta en espirales de serpiente,
O se dobla como un loto bajo el sol.

¿Qué nos dice en sus solemnes movimientos?
¿Qué nos cuentan sus menudos pasos lentos?
¿Qué oriental historia es esta de la danza.
Que al abrir la media luna de sus ojos
Se dijera traspasada en los abrojos
Como pobre mariposa su esperanza?

¿Es tristeza? ¿Es alegría lo que siente?
¿Qué misterio perfumado del Oriente,
Qué divino mago rito religioso
Desenvuelve como en ondas de un aroma
Esta flor, esta mujer, esta paloma,
Con el ritmo de su cuerpo cadensioso?

El tan-tan os lo dirá. Su prometido,
El que sabe de sus besos, se ha partido
Y la pobre gueisha ignora donde está;
Se partió en busca de glorias y fortuna
En la noche sin luceros y sin luna;
      ¿Volverá? ¿No volverá?

Lo pregunta a los luceros tembladores.
Alas brisas, a los cedros, a las flores,
Al encaje que se rompe sobre el mar;
Y pues nadie sabe a dónde fué el amado,
Esta gueisha del amor infortunado,
      ¿Qué ha de hacer, sino llorar?

Lo pregunta al huracán de nubes rotas,
A las auras, a las pálidas gaviotas,
A los cerros de esmeralda y de zafir;
Y pues nadie sabe nada del querido,
Esta gueisha del amor adolorido,
      ¿Qué ha de hacer, sino morir?

Sí. Las flautas y la gueisha están muriendo
Son suspiros y son perlas que cayendo
Forman sones, forman lágrimas divinas,
Mientras vuelve a resonar el gong sonoro,
Se disipa la visión de rosa y oro.
Y se cierran, lentamente, las cortinas. (*Mi casa* 127-29).

[8] This poem is included in the appendix to Donoso's article "*Los pájaros de fuego*. Japón y el holocausto filipino en la obra de Jesús Balmori" (234-35).

[9]
> Una música rara de flautas y platillos,
> Retumba bajo el ruido metálico de un gon;
> Se alza un telón de pájaros y soles amarillos
> Y bajo una ola inmensa de policromos brillos
> Surge ella en una lenta, gentil genuflexión.
>
> Es pálida. Su carne de nácares ignotos
> O de oro de la luna formada fue tal vez;
> Dijérase caída de ensueños florinotos
> Porque su cuerpo es vaso de perfumados lotos
> Y son como dos perlas sus mal calzados pies.
>
> Avanza. Triunfan todas sus líneas y sus galas
> En diáfano glorismo de pedrería y tul,
> Y mientras los aplausos retiemblan por las salas
> Sus brazos se alzan lentos, como si fueran alas
> Y van volando sedas de púrpura y de azul.
>
> Nos va a contar un cuento, veréis; un cuento de esos
> Que alguno fue a narrarla en el paterno hogar
> Mientras despertaban sus flores los cerezos,
> Cuando ella aún ignoraba que cosa eran los besos
> Y que cosa era otra divina cosa, amar.

Lo va a contar cantando. Oíd. Pausa. Otra pausa.
La rosa de su boca empieza:

El mandarín
Viejo y libidinoso y feo, fue la causa
De que la linda niña de la Isla Nishitausa

De fango matizara sus hojas de jazmín.
Cedióla el loco abuelo a cambio de algún oro
Que calme de sake su abrasadora sed,
En tanto ella bebía el vino de su lloro
Y el mandarín le amaba babeándola: ¡te adoro!
¡Oh pecesillo de oro que cautivó mi sed!
¡Ay!, que asco por las gemas, los oros y las flores,
Las rosas y los lazos de su pagoda real.
¡Qué miedo sus ojitos de líbricos fulgores!
¡Qué horror la tibia cámara de incienso en resplandores

Donde es un ara el lecho de sedas y coral!
En una noche llena de estrellas, la cautiva
Cargó de opio la pipa del viejo mandarín,
Y huyó sin tan siquiera saber a dónde iba.
Huyó de aquella llama donde la echaron viva
Y se perdió en las sombras flotantes del jardín.
Y nunca ya encontráronla. Jamás su paso incierto
Guió su ignota ruta, su trémulo pasar,
Que en vano la creyeron flor rota por el huerto
Y en vano en las sospechas de que se hubiera muerto
Batieron las sonoras espumas de la mar.

¿Qué se hizo de la niña de la Isla Nishitausa?...
(Su voz en la pregunta tiembla. El gon está llorando)
¿Qué se hizo de la niña del mandarín por causa?
¿Qué se hizo de la niña?...
                    (Hay una larga pausa.
El gon sigue llorando).
                    Ella, en tanto, se va.

Se va. Han tremolado todas sus líneas y sus galas
Como un loto que un beso pusiera en confusión,
Y mientras los aplausos retiemblan por las salas
Sus manos se alzan lentas como si fueran olas
¡Y van volando besos bajo el temblor del gon! (234-35).

10 "Un hombre se embriaga, como lo he hecho yo, por dolor, por no te importe qué miserias humanas, débil, cobarde á resistir el golpe á pié firme; y un hombre vá á comprar una hora de amor cuando no tiene en el mundo quien le quiera, cuando está solo y le dá pavor su soledad, cuando con hambre y sed de besos, no le importa si la boca que ha de dárselos es santa ó demonia. Esto no lo comprenden los hartos, los graves que van campanuda y pomposamente gritando ¡Moral!... ¡Puah, moral! Yo sé de muchos de estos señorones cosas enormes, cosas que publicadas darían asco hasta á los perros" (140).

11 "—Nada más sucio, nada más ridículo que la moral de los hombres" (141).

12 "Se disputaban la ducha; á Margarita se le abrió un hombro de la camisa; surgió un seno redondo, erecto, como una bola de billar, moreno bajo el pezoncito rojo, como una fresa: Ángela le puso la mano encima, apretándolo; ella saltó, sin poder abrir los ojos llenos de espuma de jabón" (58).

13   "Empeñó en acalorada discusión con la tía hablando mal de los Jesuitas. —Unos gandules, créame usted, unos hipócritas; hasta ahora nos hacen todo el daño que pueden" (31).

14   "—¿Que no había asnos, hombre? —No señora, los frailes datan de la edad media solamente" (275).

15   "Ventura bajo la lámpara eléctrica leía vagamente el 'Azul' de Darío; parecíanle los encantados versos calentura también, calentura como la de Angela, de besos" (20).

16   "Y Rafael ante Leonarda pudorosa, jadeante, dulcísima, se preguntaba si fué un sueño aquéllo de la sala, y si fué él quien palpó y besó el cuerpo supremo de la divina chiquilla encantadora" (42).

17   "[The verses] constituyen el reconocimiento por parte de un ciudadano filipino de la superioridad de los emperadores de Japón y, en consecuencia, de la autoridad del Imperio Japonés en Asia" (Introducción XXXV).

18   "Todos los dioses japoneses que forman la extraña mitología del Imperio, la dorada leyenda, el primer jalón del trono. Porque Izanami, ardiente y enamorada, siguió gestando después de su gran parto geográfico. Y surgieron, con el tiempo, Amaterazu, diosa del sol. Y su hermano Susanoo, dios del valor, que se desposaron a su vez, y de cuyas noches delirantes de pasión descienden los Emperadores del Japón" (*Los pájaros* 15).

19   "Japón era espíritu de dioses encarnados en fibras de 'shogunes,' 'samurais' y 'daimios'. ¿Por qué no le dejaban avanzar sin que una potencia blanca le cerrara el paso?" (43).

20 "Japón es un pueblo que ama a los niños, a las flores, a los ciervos, a las aguas y a los pájaros; que tiene por única y verdadera religión, el honor, y por único y verdadero altar, la patria; que no le importa sacrificar la vida y la hacienda por la vida y la gloria de su imperio; que está llamado, por su fuerza terrible y su espíritu indomable, a ser el dueño del Pacífico, el amo del Oriente, el soberano de la nueva Asia..." (42).

21 "—¡A China hay que tratarla así! A China la están civilizando como se merece y quiere, a cañonazos" (21).

22 "—No hay un japonés que no la mire como a su propia tierra. ¿Qué diferencia puede haber? Un día llegará, señor, en que todo el Oriente, toda el Asia, formará un solo pueblo, un solo grande Imperio...." (16).

23 "La primera nación del mundo" (29).

24 "Don Lino, al igual que varios ricachones filipinos, no simpatizaba con los americanos, ni estaba conforme con su política de independizar al país. . . . La independencia suponía la ruina del pueblo filipino. Sólo podían desearla los cuatro encumbrados títeres a quienes pudiera beneficiar. Al pueblo, no. El pueblo no estaba, ni estaría en mucho tiempo preparado para tan grande responsabilidad" (134).

25 "Y poderosos como eran, disimulando el oro de las cadenas con guirnaldas de flores, nos ataron las manos. Cadenas de oro, pero al fin, ¡cadenas! Entonces perdimos lo mejor que nos había dado Dios, ¡la libertad! Y desde entonces velamos en la noche y el día expiando el momento de poder romper los grillos. Por eso cayó el poeta, cantando ante la muerte. Y Bonifacio lanzando el grito de independencia" (56).

[26] "—¿Eh, Fernando, eres tú? ¡Que Dios y Filipinas te bendigan! ¡Y cuando te encuentres frente a ésos, no perdones ni a uno, mata a todos los que puedas! ¡La piedad no se ha hecho para ellos! ¡Dios no nos ha dado el corazón para arrojárselo a las fieras...!" (145).

[27] As José Donoso and Rocío Ortuño explain, the Japanese invasion of the Philippines is also addressed in several other Spanish-language, Philippine, testimonial works, including Manuel del Val's (Madval) Las estrellas vencen al sol (finished in 1946); Mariano L. de la Rosa's novel Fíame (Filipinas-América) (1946); Antonio López de Olaguer's El terror amarillo en Filipinas (1947); José G. Reyes's Terrorismo y redención. Casos concretos de atrocidades cometidas por los japoneses en Filipinas (1947); Alfredo Roa's De aquella tragedia: episodios de la última guerra en Filipinas (1947); José María Cuenco's Memorias de un refugiado (1947); Raymundo Kagahastian's Idealismo o patriotismo (1950); Benigno del Río's Siete días en el infierno: en manos de la Gestapo nipona (1950); María Paz-Zamora-Mascuñana's "Nuestros cinco últimos días bajo el yugo nipón," included in Cuentos cortos 1919-1923 y recuerdos de la Liberación 1945 (1960); and Juan Labrador's A Diary of the Japanese Occupation, written in Spanish but only published in English translation in 1989 (Ortuño 294).

[28] Unlike Tremendist authors, however, Balmori does not focus on people with disabilities or on marginal characters such as prostitutes, criminals.

[29] "Luego pasaron revista a la servidumbre, metiéndose cada uno en una habitación con una criada. A través de los elegantes dormitorios vibraban los lamentos de las fámulas ultrajadas en estrépito de vasos y botellas rotas y los gritos de los conquistadores comentando a carcajadas el vil desenvolvimiento de la hazaña. Banzai Nippon" (150).

30 "Con toda suerte de ciudadanos bestialmente torturados y fusilados luego bajo el menor pretexto" (154).

31 "¿Aliados? ¿Hombres de una misma raza? ¡Jamás! Los filipinos no descendían de piratas asiáticos. No tenían sus aborígenes en guerreros salvajes de mujeres esclavas y culto hipócrita a las sombras de los muertos y la imagen de la muerte. La sangre que corría en nuestras venas no era amarilla como el pus y la bilis, sino roja, roja, sangre de hombre, sangre de pueblo, sangre de Dios" (167).

32 "Y Fernando pudo ver, antes de cerrar el balcón, horrorizado, cómo una infeliz mujer cayendo de rodillas ante un soldado japonés, sostenía en alto el cuerpecito de su hijo, clamando misericordia. El japonés le arrebató el niño ensartándolo en su bayoneta, lo arrojó muerto contra las piedras y luego disparó contra la infortunada" (208).

33 "En el caso de Filipinas, la estética del Modernismo será el vehículo fundamental en la creación de una estética propia que contenga un ideario político basado en la idea de nación" (Introducción XVIII).

34 See my article "From Self-Orientalization to Revolutionary Patriotism: Paterno's Subversive Discourse hidden in Romances."

35 "Precisamente por estos motivos de compromiso político y búsqueda de una identidad nacional, el Modernismo en Filipinas adquirirá una personalidad propia que se traducirá en la idealización de la filipinidad" (Introducción XIII).

³⁶ Regarding the Orientalism displayed among many influential Latin American writers, it must be said that they often just felt curiosity and attraction for Asian countries, seeing them as a source of a new, alternative knowledge; usually, they did not advocate for hegemonic domination in that continent.

³⁷ "Porque España no debía ser extraña a nuestra suerte. Tal que en un manto inmenso de luz, ella nos había envuelto en una civilización que amalgamada al cabo de tres siglos con la importada por América, hizo de nuestro pueblo lo que ningún otro pueblo del Oriente pudo ser, y nos formó una raza de hombres fuertes, aptos, dignos. España puso los cimientos formidables de nuestra estructura nacional y América coronó más tarde el edificio con sus modernas galas y sus adornos prácticos. A las dos les debía Filipinas su orgulloso pasado y su triunfal presente" (27).

³⁸ "No, no habían venido los japoneses a darnos la libertad, de la que estábamos sobrados, ni a darnos nada que no fueran el hambre, la destrucción y la muerte" (168).

³⁹ "¿Y de qué libertad que nos haya podido conceder el Japón te atreves a hablar tú, si Filipinas era cuando la atacasteis más libre que fue nunca y puede ser jamás Japón?" (195).

⁴⁰ "Don Lino cogió los pliegos y a su vez, los empezó a examinar. Había tenido a su servicio, como jardineros, a un par de hombres conspicuos. Porque Otta resultaba capitán de la marina de guerra japonesa. Y Kenjiro, comandante de las fuerzas imperiales" (58).

Manila, Philippines was declared an open city on 26 Dec 1941 to prevent unnecessary destruction.
Source: U.S. Dept. of the Army
Retrieved from: https://ww2db.com/image.php?image_id=4244

BIRDS OF FIRE
A Filipino War Novel

Jesús Balmori

Proem

All the pages of this book, except for the last chapter, were written during the Japanese occupation. They were miraculously preserved because they were hidden inside glass jars that I buried in the garden of my house. The repeated assaults made by the Japanese henchmen to seize the book were in vain. Lilies bloomed every day on the ground where the book was hidden. And the good God watched over it with his divine mercy.

New Manila,
Quezon City.
Year 1945.

PART I

I

When Don Lino Robles came down the final steps of the luxurious staircase, the first thing he noticed, in the distance, through the foliage and the morning mist, was two Japanese men bent over a bed of chrysanthemums.

Astonishing people! No one could transform the most emaciated tree trunks and the most abominable roots into leafy trees and marvelous flowers as well as they could. In less than a year, they had converted the four thousand meters of uncultivated land surrounding his palatial mansion into a garden of enchantment, with water fountains, pagodas, golden bridges over tiny lakes where pompous storks winged their way, shattering the stems of lotus flowers, green blades that displayed at their tip a chalice of nacre or rose. It had been a miracle of Philippine land, warm and fertile, ready to change into fruit and flower at every instant. And it had been an unheard of effort by this pair of expert little men, true artists, who supervised a few native workers to accomplish such a miracle. Going down the paths lined with flowers, moist with dew at the break of day, little trails filled with the fragrance of newly cut grass, Don Lino approached the gardeners.

"Good morning."

They both stood up from their bent legs, and made deep, ceremonial bows.

"Good morning, sir."

The gentleman offered them cigarettes. Kenjiro, the eldest, placed his behind one ear. Otta, being more democratic, put it in his mouth and began to chew it. In the meantime, Don Lino filled his eyes and his spirit with the superb beauty of the flowering branches. At his feet swirled an emerald cloak, honeycombed with petals of all colors, as though they were captive butterflies, as though they were rubies and opals and pearls and sapphires from an enormous broken necklace, fallen into pieces over the grass. And not only here, in this corner, but all along the pathways, around the pagodas, climbing through the trees and through the arches, on every side, everywhere, flowers.

Finally, Don Lino stopped contemplating them. And turning to the yellow men, he began to speak. He liked being with these people. He got along well with them, and he admired their ways. He had made several trips to Japan, the last one not long ago, following the death of his wife. His daughter, Natalia, was finishing her studies at a secondary school in Manila. His boy, Fernando, had taken charge of his large estate in the north of Luzón. He was a poet, and he loved the countryside. He had acknowledged it in a Sonnet to a beautiful village girl: "The countryside has been made for the flowers, like you. And for the poets and the birds…"

In Don Lino's opinion, Japan was an exceptional country. And at this moment, in the presence of this lush Japanese flora that spilled its hues and its aromas of an Asiatic censer at his feet, listening to the obsequious, lyrical words of its men, and stunned by the incessant flight of sparrows in the foliage, he longed affectionately for the powerful Empire.

Flowers and birds reminded him of its divine origin. In its genteel beginnings, the gods were unaware of love until a winged pair, as they mated among the flowers, awakened life to love. The god was Izanagi and the goddess, his wife and sister, the beautiful Izanami,[1] from whose loins sprung forth the Japanese islands, all the Japanese gods that made up the strange mythology of the Empire, the golden legend, the first milestone of the throne. For Izanami, ardent and in love, continued to conceive after her great geographical birthing. And in time there emerged Amaterasu,[2] the sun goddess. And her brother, Susanoo,[3] god of courage, and they in turn married, and from their delirious nights of passion are descendants the Emperors of Japan. First of them all, Jimmu-tennō.[4]

"Where are you from, Otta?"

"From Nikko,[5] sir; the city with the golden temples."

"And you, Kenjiro?"

"I was born in Nara, sir, like the sacred deer.[6] Only I grew up in Kamakura,[7] on the green hill, at the feet of the Daibutsu."[8]

The sun was beginning to burn hot in a cloudless sky. Don Lino sought the shade of an old palm tree to continue talking:

"I know those places; I've seen them. They are so lively and beautiful: don't you miss them?"

Kenjiro and Otta smiled enigmatically, as they gave each other side-long glances. Behind the affected humility, one could sense the throbbing of the immense pride of their race.

And Otta said:

"This land here is as good as ours could be."

Kenjiro added:

"There is no Japanese who doesn't see it as their own land. What difference could there be? The day will come, sir, when all the Orient, all of Asia, will be one people, one great Empire..."

Natalia interrupted them, approaching, wrapped in youth and sunshine:

"Where are you, Papa? Where have you gone off to?"

Don Lino guided her with his voice:

"Here, over here, don't break my lilies...! Oh, look what these fellows have done! Have you ever seen such beautiful chrysanthemums?"

Hanging onto her father's arm, Natalia barely glanced at the flowers. She was a modern young girl, practical, very American in style, a devotee of sports and sensible things. Nothing to do with dreams or romanticism. Poetry? The movies? Dance? Flowers? Well, flowers weren't bad, but she preferred oranges, apples...

She had a boyfriend and went on walks alone or to dances with him. He was a doctor and advertised himself in the press as a specialist in every kind of illness in the Universities of Tokyo, Berlin and Vienna. But in spite of his claims, he had no patients. He pinned his hopes of having a successful life on a marriage with Natalia and the millions of her father.

"Shall we go inside for breakfast, Papa?"

They walked slowly back to the house. The Nipponese[9] remained behind, yellow silhouettes among the yellow of the chrysanthemums, again bent over the ground under a fiery sun like the one on their flags. Seated at the table in the spacious, elegant dining room, Fernando, smoking a cigarette and taking small sips from his coffee cup, sat up part way when he noticed his father's presence.

"How are you, Papa?"

"Feeling stronger every day, son. You'll have to write a serenade of verses to my sixty years. They weigh less on me than sixty feathers."

The son smiled:

"You can't grow old. For men like you, the years go by like the leaves of a tree floating through the air, without leaving a trace. You are a man with the best, most gentle nature that's ever existed. Your entire life is sheer optimism. You are a wise man, Papa, if not a philosopher. From your chalice, the same chalice that all men drink from, what is gall and vinegar for everyone else, turns to wine and honey for you."

Natalia, sitting next to the old man, was putting cream and sugar in his coffee, and stirring the cup with a spoon. As Fernando looked at her, light-skinned, pale, emerging from the green, delicate silk of her "slacks," she seemed like a lily rising out of its stem. On her face, round like a full moon, her slanted eyes appeared to be asleep. Small mouth, thin lips and dazzling white teeth. A mound of hair, dark and abundant, fell in unnatural curls over her forehead and her shoulders. She was thin, small, nervous...

"And me, what about me, Fernando? Don't you have any bouquets for me?"

"So, are you feeling like a flower this morning?"

Don Lino interrupted them:

"Speaking of those, take a walk around the garden later on. The chrysanthemums are in bloom. You're going to see them in all their beauty."

"The bulbs from Nagasaki?"

"The very ones. See how they take root in our soil!"

Don Ramon, Don Lino's only brother and a few years older, burst brashly into the room.

"Have you heard yet? Have you heard about the catastrophe that's in the making?"

"No, man. What's happening?"

"Haven't you read the morning papers?"

"Not yet, but tell us, Ramon! What's going on?"

Don Ramon pulled up a chair, sat down and, visibly upset, held out a newspaper that he was brandishing like a threat:

"Take this, read it, there on the front page, those letters a mile high..."

And Don Lino read the headlines out loud:

"Germany has declared war on France." "England is preparing to declare war on Germany." "All of Europe heading for a new bloodbath."

And he refused to read any further or learn any more details. He laid the paper down on the table, and turned to his brother:

"All right, let them clobber each other! What's that got to do with us?"

Don Ramon trembled in his fury:

"What do you mean, this has nothing to do with us? With this new war, we could lose a lot, and we could even get involved in the Holocaust if God doesn't help us."

"Calm down, Ramon, calm down. This war can bring us money. We could sell all sorts of produce that would just go to waste in our storehouse, with no market for it. The Germans, the French and the English are a long way away from the Philippines. Besides, we have America to protect us. And who's going to pick a fight with America? Who would dare to provoke the United States?"

"Supposing that nobody would provoke them, do you think they would settle for twiddling their thumbs in a war that's trying to overturn democracy? The United States will get involved, and they'll have every right to, because without their intervention, freedom in the world would just turn into a fairy-tale. Because with their colossal power and force, they would pulverize the four bandits who dream of dividing up the world; and because wherever there arises a victim of despotism and barbarity, there will be America, lifting up the fallen and punishing the oppressor."

"Bunk!"

"Bunk...? Pay attention to what I'm going to tell you. This war that's breaking out in Europe today will be a war in America, Africa, Asia and Oceania tomorrow. There's great ambition and enormous force involved. Japan..."

Don Lino sat up, holding back his laughter:

"Now it's Japan! The inevitable bogeyman! The perpetual threat! The horrendous nightmare...!"

"Japan will declare war on America. And the Philippines will be attacked by Japan."

"Because you say so!"

"Because the facts will speak for me!"

"You can rest easy, Ramon. And even keep dreaming out loud, if that's what keeps you worried and frightens you. I know Japan and its dreams of conquest. Honorable people. A country of noble traditions and enormous politeness. They won't be a part of the universal 'gangsterism!' They won't get involved with anybody!"

"No, huh? And China?" thundered Don Ramon.

"You have to deal with China like that. They're civilizing China the way she deserves and wants, with artillery fire. China went out looking for what's happening to it, and a lot more than what's happening to it."

"Oh, yes? Well, bon appétit, Don Lino." He was leaving. He didn't want to stay there and listen to such nonsense. He would remember his words sooner or later. "Goodbye."

He left in a huff, and his brother couldn't stop him, but he was followed by Fernando...

"Uncle, don't be this way, don't go away like this..."
"And how do you expect me to leave, singing?"
"It's just that Papa..."
"Tell your papa to go to... Japan!"
He wouldn't be stopped.

Impossible to stop him. Fernando went to his room, and from his balcony he looked out over the garden. On the other side of the trees and the flowers was the boulevard, and beyond the boulevard the sea, brilliant and pulsing. In the clear airiness, birds, seemingly made of silver, flew very high.

"Oh, blue sky! Oh, blue sea of Ermita,[10] majestic and beautiful. Could those birds, like the ones that, on the flowery branch of a cherry tree taught Asian gods about love, could they someday turn into birds of hate, into birds of fire that would plunge us into ruin, into death, into pain..."

III

His first ladylove was the moon.

He had just turned six years old, and when the nanny showed it to him, softly glowing among the clouds, she had him believe that it was an enchanted princess wandering lost in the night, dressed in silver, and with a star for a crown.

Later, as he was growing up, he realized that the nanny was lying, and he stopped loving the fantastic princess. The truth about life began to light up his road. And he began to feel the need that every man has, from his very youngest years, to love a woman. Natalia's little girl friends, with their dresses down to the calves of their legs, and their tiny braids gathered with colored ribbons, began to feel the darts of his amorous precociousness. With essences taken from the little bottles on his mother's dressing table, he perfumed the paper of the messages he sent to Lulu, Margot, Chito and Nena. In them he promised he would go mad, die from love, using red colored ink, under the drawing of a wounded heart, his own. In point of fact, what was truly wounded and bloody was his syntax and spelling.

He was every bit a man in short pants. Every bit a Don Juan with a book of grammar under his arm. And since there was no lack of girls to give in to his passionate demands and stop him from dying, he spent his time writing verses to them instead of learning his algebra lessons.

He hated his schoolwork. To hell with Physics and Greek. Rhetoric was the only thing that deserved any respect. Everything else was reading "The Thousand and One Nights," books of adventure by Salgari,[11] and the fantastic tales of Jules Verne.

He loved his mother while she was alive. He adored her, as though instead of being a woman, she were a Saint bestowing all favors and all love on him. He imagined her walking in the heavens instead of on the ground, above the highest and bluest skies. He thought of his father as the greatest man on earth. And he loved Natalia with tender, solicitous affection, overlooking her free, headstrong character, believing it his duty as an elder brother to protect her, indulge her, watch over her.

His father let him do what he wanted without worrying about the future. If he didn't want to study, then don't do it! The country was full of professionals who did nothing but go around being nuisances. Robles, with his vast properties and his millions in the Bank, had more than taken care of the future of his children.

But when he really did begin to grow into a man, he felt the need to busy himself at something. And he began to devote his time to the running of the estate, which Don Lino left in the hands of administrators. He loved the land, the good mother, the blessed treasure. He was captivated by the sight of the fields, rolling mantles of emerald and gold; the newly ploughed furrows, the green cane and the finest sprouts. At the foot of a hill he had a rustic dwelling next to a brook that he would swim across, or along which he sculled many nights, rowing a small boat that in the glow of the stars seemed to be an enormous dreamlike fish. In addition, in the nearby town, in the manor house of the landowner, Gala, a love was waiting every passing minute for him to come.

A girl with a complexion of amber, and who smelled like a flower of the fields. A sweetly indigenous beauty, with a dreamy expression, and the languid eyes of a slave girl. An only daughter, her parents wanted to keep her by their side forever. And she was raised at home, in her town, in the holy love of God, and in the simplicity and virtue of country traditions. He had formalized the relations with her, and they were ready to be married. Because of that, the Gala family had moved to the capital, and they were living in Santamesa, in a small villa surrounded by a grove of trees. He went to see her there every day, and he was driving there right now in his automobile.

It was just that he had to stop when he was about to turn onto the boulevard. The first division of a great military parade was coming, in honor of the anniversary of the Commonwealth. He stopped the car at the side of the road and waited for the procession. A band playing military music soon appeared in the center of the road, with a noisy crowd pressing along both sides. Then came the flags, the white, red and blue colors trembling in the breeze. Afterward, on horseback, the Chief of Staff. And then, the troops, valiant, proud, their swords and bayonets flashing in the sun. One thousand, two thousand, thousands of men.

Our soldiers were marching along with the American troops. They were the guardians of our honor, the defenders of the country. Someday, perhaps, many of them would fall, bloodied, in defending these flags that they now carried on high, whipping together, their folds commingling, kissing the wind like two lovers. Fernando got out of his car, and making his way through the crowd, he walked toward

Luneta Park. The President was speaking. From a distance, he heard him addressing the people from atop an improvised platform. Declarations about a possible war, and about America and the Philippines. Emphasizing his words, he was saying that the country needed to prepare itself to confront all kinds of battles and sacrifices. And even more, he said that at any moment the Philippines would be ready to fight alongside America to defend Democracies and to die beside America if need be, to give our lives for the liberty of the world.

At that moment Fernando thought that uncle Ramon hadn't been talking through his hat, saying that a catastrophe was coming. When the very President of the nation was warning us like this of the danger...!

The mass of humanity, spilling out after the ceremony was over, dragged him along, pushing him forward. And suddenly, at the mercy of that tumultuous surge, he found himself in front of the monument to Legazpi[12] and Urdaneta.[13] Oh, blessed Friar! Oh, brave captain. What would they say if you suddenly came back to life? What would they say if that bronze could speak, and if they knew that the Cross and the sword that they handed down to us as their greatest legacy and their greatest love was being threatened by powerful hidden enemies?

Because Spain could not ignore our fate. Since it has enveloped us with an immense cloak of light, in a civilization which, at the end of three centuries, blended with the one from America, made of our population what no other people from the Orient could be, forming us into a race of strong, capable, admirable men. Spain laid the formidable foundation of our national framework, and later on America crowned the structure with its modern regalia and practical adornments. The Philippines was indebted to both of them for its proud past and its triumphant present. They both had the right to look back into their history and toward their future. Especially America with which we are united by bonds of Government and the eternal and enormous gratitude of a liberty that cost us only the asking and only the wish: very different from other people, from all peoples, from the Americans themselves who had to win their liberty with gunfire. Shoulder to shoulder with them, all citizens, like our Chieftains, like our soldiers. Then let anyone come to attack us and try to conquer us. Because knowing how to be peaceful and with humble hearts while we lived free and happy, if we were to see our land trampled and our liberty scorned, we would learn how to kill, we would know how to die.

 Evening was falling and the electric candelabra lining the walkway were turning on, creating a pearly light. Fernando went to find his car. He had been delayed for at least an hour. A certain genteel princess would be anxiously waiting for him.

 He arrived in fifteen minutes. She was waiting for him behind the garden gate. In the deep shadows he nearly didn't see her. Not her or the boughs of roses surrounding her. He noticed only her perfume, the sweet perfume, of the roses, of the woman...

 "Oh, Marta!"

 How beautiful it is, while thinking about death, to be able to talk about love. How voluptuous it is, among the flowers, to feel the excited heart of the woman we love, beating against our chest. And how the stars appear at night to see a man and a woman kissing on the earth...!

 "Marta...! Marta...!"

 Without letting go their hands, as though they were afraid of becoming lost in an abyss, they made their way to the chalet, guided by the glow of the newly lit lamps. On the veranda, veiled by a curtain of climbing plants, they came upon Doña Claudia and Don Eladio Gala. She resembled her daughter; she was another Marta, nineteen years older. He was a hardy, virile chap, tanned by the sun in the fields, energized by the mountain air.

Fernando explained why he was late. He had been detained by the military parade. The President had been at Luneta Park, speaking about the reasons for a likely war. Everyone was talking about the war. People were waiting for the United States to become involved, and the Japanese would take advantage of the situation to get up to their old tricks.

"I don't think Japan would risk taking any action like that," remarked Don Eladio.

"Neither do I," Fernando went on, "but Papa, who was the first to laugh when the discussion came up at home a few weeks ago, has started to change his mind. The lightning quick victories by the Nazis, and Italy getting into the fight, are beginning to have an effect on the way he thinks. And you know Papa, and what a fanatical Japanophile he is. Japan isn't just a first-rate powerhouse. For him, it's the greatest country in the world."

"But is Asia the world?"

"The debates he has with Uncle Ramon are incredible – about imperialism and the democracies, and about who is who, and when all's said and done, which one is going to end up with their hands on their heads. Worse than that is when they argue in front of Natalia's music teacher, who's Italian, and Kauffman, the family doctor, who is German. And then you should see how poor Ramon is, fighting against Japan, Italy and Germany."

"God keep us from evil like that," prayed Doña Claudia, as she stood up.

"As you say, Claudia," whispered Don Eladio, standing up as well.

The two sweethearts were left alone, close together, looking into each other's eyes, as they both leaned back together in the settee. She gave off a faint, pure aroma that swathed her completely, from her untwined hair down to her bare feet.

"How I love you, Marta!"

"And don't I love you too?"

He caressed her hands laden with bracelets, and playing lightly with her rings, he made the diamonds and opals turn on her fingers...

"And when we are married, when you are mine alone, I'll love you twice as much, forever, just the way I could love only my mother, the way you deserve to be loved!"

A woman at last, she allowed herself to have doubts:

"All our lives, Nando?"

"Even beyond our lives!"

"Even if I get ugly? Even when I'm an old woman? No matter what happens? No matter what?"

He continued to caress her:

"Would you stop loving me because of that?"

She protested, withdrawing her hands, trembling as she sat up.

"Never!"

"Not for anything in the world? Not for anything that happens in our lives?"

"Never!"

He put his arms around her and kissed her on the lips.

"Marta! Marta!"

She seemed to grow faint in his arms, like a wounded bird, throbbing, like burning incense that is dying out. Her eyes half-closed and her lips half-parted from love, there was not one petal of her flower-like flesh that was not filled with love. Completely yielding and surrendering to love, she offered herself to him like a chalice of honey.

"Take me! Consume me!" she seemed to cry out, while sighing and sobbing. "Let my life's blood warm your veins. Let the essence of my soul refresh you throughout your life."

IIII

"If there exists a paradise in this world, that paradise is called the Philippines."

That is what Signore Bruno Anselmi proclaimed to the four winds. He was a professor of singing and pianoforte, born in Milan, and was extremely popular in Manila's artistic circles and music academies.

He had lived in the country for a number of years, and the eminent professor had visited the main islands. For him Luzón, Visayas[14] and Mindanao were marvelous, but not as great as Garibaldi,[15] Mussolini[16] and Verdi.[17] As for its people, that was something else; there was a lot to say about that. In his opinion, the Filipinos were only passably civilized.

When one of his students was singing a ballad and gave out with a squawk, that was when the Signore Anselmi cried loudest about the ineptness of our people. Just a little brighter than the Ethiopians. If the Philippines were a dependency of Italy instead of having as its sovereign the United States, the tenors would never be off pitch. And the pretty, well-heeled young women would marry Italians to improve the race.

He had come very early to the home of the Robles under the pretext of giving Natalia a singing lesson. She had quarreled with her boyfriend the night before, and instead of singing, she was shrieking. Anselmi was breaking into a cold sweat and seething in front of the piano, shaking with indignation.

"Per la mare de Dio, signorina Natalia. Per la santa mare de Cristoforo Colombo."

"What's the matter?"

What she was doing wasn't singing. She was making a martyr of the notes and the sounds.

"Well, if I'm not singing, let Caruso[18] do it."

"Ma, Caruso doesn't have to learn the song. It's you, you..."

All right, some other day. She was in no mood for music right now. Her chest was hurting, her throat hurt, her head hurt...

"Santa Madonna!"

"Ora pronobis!"

She left him alone, a head-case, collapsed on the piano bench, and went into her room, slamming the door loudly. Hearing the disturbance, Don Lino came out to the drawing room to calm the professor down. He could picture the scene. It was something that happened frequently. Oh, the artists!

"What happened, maestro?"

"La sua bambina, Don Lino, she takes divine art as a joke. Too bad. She could become a diva! When she wants to, she sings like an angel. And when she doesn't want, she screams as if she's in a dentist's office."

"That's just the way with girls, maestro. You need to be patient with little girls. They're almost all the very picture of impertinence."

Ma, Natalia was a pain. If she would apply herself, if she would learn, she would be able to sing "Madame Butterfly." She had a beautiful voice. She had the temperament. She had the gift. She had...

Don Lino cut short the praises to his daughter.

"What news do you have of your country? How is the battle going?"

Anselmi spun around on his bench, visibly moved. The strings of his heart had been touched most powerfully. With his beautiful baritone voice, he began to speak robustly, heartily and warmly:

"Oh, my dear Don Lino! The war was coming along just the way it should, with Germany taking over Europe. With the help of the Italians, it would be decisive. You should see what a man Mussolini was! You should just see that fellow!"

And to Don Lino's consternation, he continued:

"My uncle. The cousin of mia mare!"

Anselmi was not supposed to be an artist, a musician. His father, Count Blardoni, had planned another life for him more in harmony with his class and his lineage. He wanted him to become a magistrate, a General, a Prince of the Church, something very different and much loftier than what he had turned out to be...

"Ma, I rebelled, and I escaped from the palace in Florence where we lived. And I went wandering around the world, singing, until I ended up in the Philippines. Because I felt art running through my veins like a fire that was burning me up, tutta la vita. And I gave up everything for art: my family, my home, honors and riches."

Anselmi had a beautiful voice and a beautiful figure. If he hadn't hated water and had just spruced up a little more, he could have turned into a real heartthrob of the opera. But he was absolutely messy and slovenly. And this took away all the other good qualities about his figure.

He continued to pontificate in front of Don Lino who was now beginning to have doubts about his amusing tale of being a Prince Charming:

"Ma, I'm not sorry, no. Because I know that as far as my singing goes, Tita Rufo[19] is just a putz compared to me. And next to me, the best professore is nothing but a cat clawing at the piano keys. Oh, if instead of being here, dillydallying around out of love for the country and for you, I were in my beautiful homeland, or in Vienna, or in Paris, the greatest men would come to render me their esteem, and the most noble duchesses would drown in perfumed letters."

Meanwhile, from her room, Natalia was bellowing out the Serenata of Toselli.[20] Anselmi pretended that the mockery didn't reach his ears. With difficulty, Don Lino held back his laughter. Until suddenly Fernando burst into the room, followed by Doctor Fritz von Kauffman.

"What's going on, Lino? What's the matter? Fernando tells me that you had a rough night."

"My cough."

"Bronchitis. Take care of yourself, fellow. Don't smoke so much. Especially those American cigarettes…"

The Italian saw his opportunity to make a dignified escape to someplace else with his music. And making a gesture like Radamés[21] onstage, he took his leave ceremoniously. Oh, that little joker, he grumbled as he was leaving, what a way to abuse someone, just because she was extremely wealthy and knew that he was covertly courting her. She was absolutely ugly and stupid. But a rosy cash cow for the one who was able to win her, for him, especially the one for whom she would turn out to be a real "bocato di cardinali."[22]

In the meanwhile, he had made Don Lino swallow his little fairy tale. The son of a count; the nephew of il Duce;[23] a hero of art; a martyr out of his love for the Philippines. Don Lino would tell his daughter. And the little joker's eyes would pop out of her head and in the future, she would stop treating him like a nobody.

Doctor Kauffman had been Don Lino's physician for a great many years. He had the reputation of being one of the best doctors in the country and had come there as a young man. Like all men of science, he was a man of few words. Despite the great trust he enjoyed in this house, he contented himself with giving his patient an injection without asking for or offering any explanations. He was always in a hurry. He would come back in two days.

Don Lino, Fernando and Natalia – who had returned to the living room after Anselmi disappeared – were left alone.

"What did the doctor tell you, Papa?"

Running his fingertips over the part of his arm that still stung from the shot, he said laboriously:

"You need to be careful with the maestro and treat him with more respect. It turns out that he's the nephew of none other than the Duce. And besides that, he's the nephew of I don't know how many counts."

Natalia burst out laughing:

"Of the Conte Verde, Papa. The ship that Sandoval came back from Europe on."

"So Anselmi is the Duce's nephew?" asked Fernando.

"That's what he just swore to me, himself."

Fernando shrugged:

"Well, if that's what he says, he's doing himself no favor."

"Why?"

Because Mussolini was a poor beggar, a miserable little schoolteacher, a lowlife, brushed off by everybody, before he became what he is in his country now. Outside of Italy he was a bum, booked by the police, and arrested more than once. And apart from all this, he was a horrible clown who was dragging a land of musicians and singers into a catastrophic war, where they would only find ruin and death.

Don Lino sat up:

"But look, what if the Axis[24] win?"

Fernando sat up straight as well:

"Don't even think of it, Papa. I'm not one to argue with you or to try to change your mind. But I follow logic in my thinking and I go by what history teaches us. They both call to mind those other great ambitions for world-wide domination, like the ones that the horsemen of the apocalypse are galloping over the world for today. What happened to them back then? They went up in smoke! And what became of those incomparable conquistadors who tried to challenge the world with the point of their sword? Dust! Barely one glorious, sad memory of an enormous effort smothered in fire, blood and tears!"

Natalia protested:

"But, enough about war! Why war? We don't talk about anything but war in this house!"

And in a change of tone:

"Papa, tonight there's a dance at the Manila Hotel in honor of the American administration. Will you allow Sandoval to take me?"

Fernando looked at her pitifully:

"You two are living and continually dancing in the crater of a volcano that is going to erupt very soon."

"And you, with that story too?"

"Me, and the whole world."

"Well, the world is wrong. Sandoval says..."
Fernando interrupted her, laughing:
"From the Universities of Tokyo, Berlin and Vienna..."
"From wherever, blast it! Sandoval says that the war will never reach us. And he knows very well what he's talking about."
And she turned around to bang away on the piano.

The room was filled with bright, happy notes, as if there were a festival with birds and fountains. Don Lino and Fernando, lost in the musical outburst, continued talking about the province at one moment, then the estate and the approaching great harvest...

The Italian musician was right. If there was one place in the world where paradise existed, that paradise was called the Philippines. Each island was like a nest warmed by peace, by well-being and happiness, where the golden spikelets of rice are seeded, the canes drip honey from their stalks, the hot broth from the fruit of the palms simmers, rising to the wind in the song of the water, the sweet water and the salt water, over the sands and the stones and the moss.

Mindanao, a Moorish princess dressed in silver and covered with pearls, reclining on a Vinta boat[25] with carved oars, fiery red sails, flags and wings of its exotic emblazonment. Visayas, soft beauty, immense lump of sugar, ballerina of the delicate "balitao"[26] dance, wrapped in its light "patadión" – a short skirt that veils its beauty the way a cloud conceals the splendor of a star. And Luzón, brilliant and powerful as a quivering lance, flesh of glory, blood of the loom and the plow and the anvil, with the scent of factories and the incense of fields and altars.

Three thousand, one hundred forty-one islands rocked by the waves of the China Sea, the Celebes Sea and the Pacific Ocean. Blazoning on high its aboriginal spirit, embellished with the most prodigious culture of the Occident and the greatest developments and virtues of the best races. The male of this Eden, his forehead bent to the good earth, blissfully gripping the handle of the plow, behind the patient carabao that is opening the furrow for the future sprout. And his sinful Eve, the dark, amorous woman, crowned by the sun and by flowers, standing over the immense crop field, with a child in her arms, her face to the sky, offering God the fruit of her heart, the new Filipino, the man of tomorrow, like a promise of redemption and glory.

IV

In his modern office library where a great bronze Buddha,[27] smiling and rotund, stood out splendidly on a lacquered pedestal, Don Lino was talking in private with his brother:

"It's not like I'm some dirty old man, you know? But keep in mind that I was left a widower at an age when a man seems to need the warmth of a female more than ever. A second boyhood is fierier than the first one, Ramon. A person starts to realize that he is drawing away from, losing, extinguishing the only thing that makes life worth living: love. And love is not Cupid, that small boy pictured with little, blue wings and a blindfold over his eyes, shooting out arrows this way and that. It's something more dignified, more serious, much more real, to my way of seeing it. Aphrodite rising from the bitter froth, with her full breasts and open arms, awaiting the man, offering herself to the male who is roaring with passion, a poor slave, fallen to his knees before her dazzling nakedness.

"I went looking for that woman! I searched for her because I needed her, because I was desperate for her, because the blood surging through my veins, was coursing strong and full..."

"And did you find that woman?"

"I found her, Ramon."

"And do you have her here now?"

"No! She stayed in that paper house, like a doll lost among the cedars and cryptomerias of Kyoto. She's from over there. Her name is Haruko San. As beautiful as a golden temple, soft as silk and the petals of flowers from a cherry tree. She made me happy with her timid, devoted love. Those women know how to love. If you ever need a loving woman at your side, look for a Japanese one!"

"Thank you!"

Don Lino lit a cigarette and offered one to his brother, and continued his story, inhaling smoke:

"That's where my great fondness for Japan and everything Japanese comes from. The best hours of my life, I've lived them there. Japan is a nation that loves children, flowers, deer, its waters and its birds; its only true altar is its homeland. It could not care less about sacrificing life and property for the life and glory of the empire. It is being called upon, by its terrible force and its indomitable spirit, to be the master of the Pacific, ruler of the Orient, the sovereign of new Asia... Are you shocked...?"

"I'm listening."

Ah, then listen well. It never took communion with white men before any tabernacle. It didn't believe in their friendship. They were a bunch of thugs, mad men, they could never even live at peace with each other. They went on the attack like wolves for the slightest reason; it was a matter of destroying themselves. Where were we going to end up with that kind of men? At any moment the world would wake up without any people on it! They would have wiped us all out!

They're provoking Japan, and sooner or later Japan will give them a bitter lesson. We're not dealing with people who are merchants or half breeds from other races who are naturalized English or

Americans. Japan was a spirit of gods involved with the fiber of "Shōguns,"[28] "Samurai,"[29] and "Daimyos."[30] Why didn't they let it advance without a white power blocking its way? Poor Magellan, when he named the greatest of the oceans the Pacific, committed the sin of being naïve. And, if not, all in good time!

Don Ramon shrugged his shoulders scornfully.

"Go on with your story about the woman."

Through the wide-open windows came the splendor of the morning, with the smell of grass and flower and the noisy chattering of the sparrows above the pageantry of the trees. Don Lino continued:

"Every now and then, I get letters from her. She is still faithful to me, she loves me, she hasn't forgotten me. The day I left her, she fell to her knees before me, silently crying, holding onto me, kissing my feet. Poor Haruko San! Poor 'musme,'[31] sweet and beloved! I left her with several thousand 'yen,' and the promise to return soon..."

"You did it splendidly. 'With bread, all griefs are lighter.'"

The sparrows were screeching as they chased each other through the branches. From outside came the sound of Natalia playing a Bach fugue on the piano.

"If Natalia gets married, if Fernando marries, I'll go back to Japan. If it weren't for them, I would be in Kyoto. My life is over there!"

"What for, Lino, what for? You don't need to go back there. Japan will come here, and they'll bring you your Japanese girl!"

He threw the cigarette into the garden, over the head of the great Buddha.

"May Guatama[32] keep you! Goodbye!"

"Are you going?"

He was leaving. He didn't want to hear any more stories. He didn't believe in Japan and its tale. The heroic divine origin of its people! Valiant pride! They were human beasts, pulling along in their little carts everyone who goes traipsing through the parks. The women, selling their caresses to thousands, to millions in the red-light district of Yoshiwara![33] And the rest, the middle classes and the so-called aristocracy, all the men, into the army, to invade lands and throttle weak races, for the honor and benefit of the empire. And in the meantime the women, to get pregnant, to give birth like machines, continually and mathematically so that the Mikado[34] will not lack hit-men, and the defenseless lands of Asia and the Orient cannot be certain that when they go to sleep at night, they won't wake up the following day under a storm of fire...! Goodbye!

"Hey now, you're spouting nonsense!"

"Goodbye!"

As he was leaving, he ran into Natalia, who was coming in, followed by the manager of the estate!

"Where are you going, Uncle?"

"To find a Japanese lady for your father!"

Natalia laughed out loud. Could her father and her uncle always be quarreling about such fantastic things?

She left the manager in Don Lino's office and went back to the living room. Awaiting her was her fiancé, the famous Doctor Sandoval.

Sandoval's face was lost behind a pair of horn-rimmed glasses so large that they might be said to be headlights on a car. His cranium was visible under a mop of hair held in place with a layer of shiny pomade. Thin, slight, nearly insignificant, he dressed in exaggeratedly American style. By his physiognomic traits, one could deduce his Chinese descent.

He was jealous, as usual, because he imagined men ate Natalia up with their eyes, and that she loved to function as their feast. It was just that now he seemed to be a little bit right. At the dance the night before, she had behaved in a scandalously mawkish fashion with a lieutenant who had just graduated from the Academy.

"Phew, a lieutenant!"

Didn't it make her feel ashamed? All the girls were laughing at her! And what a spectacle she made, dancing with that beanpole, tall and stiff as a board who, not wanting to be out of step, instead of holding her at the waist, nearly carried her around by the neck...!

"Anyway, you looked like the lieutenant's sword!"

She was accustomed to his fits of jealousy, and she paid no attention to them. She laughed and let him vent, and when she saw that he had suddenly calmed down, she began to defend herself.

He needed to sign his name as Othello.[35] He was debasing himself by being jealous of men who didn't hold a candle to him. Wasn't he ashamed of insulting her in such a disrespectful way, comparing her to some common flirt? Would she be in a relationship with him if she wasn't in love with only him, her Pepe...?

"Liar!"

"Liar? Who would stop her from leaving him flat if he wasn't more important to her than those fools he imagined were his rivals?"

Sandoval allowed himself to be convinced. Because he needed to believe her so that he could breathe easily, and because the fact was that Don Lino's money was more important to him than Natalia's faithfulness. They had gone along like this for a year, and the day she didn't make him angry felt like a day that was lacking in emotion.

"But don't you go dancing with that lieutenant again."

"Of course not."

"Don't even look him in the face."

"Of course."

"Who is he?"

"I don't know. I think his father is a Colonel."

A colonel father and a lieutenant son. The grandchild would turn out to be a sergeant. What a family. A bunch of soldiers!

"Of course!"

"This is the only country where soldiers dare to make an appearance in society. It's your fault, the fault of you girls where it's all the same to you: a guy in a dress coat, in a uniform, in a cassock. You don't see this in Europe or in America, or in any other part of the world, I tell you!"

Of course, yes, he was right! And with her fine, fragrant handkerchief she daubed a rebellious drop of perspiration on his forehead. What a way to get worked up over nothing! Were they going to spend the whole time like this? To hell with all lieutenants. She loved only him, her Pepe.

Defeated!

He kissed the drop of his own perspiration on the fine batiste, and on the fingertips of the consoling Samaritan. And he went on to talk to her softly and gently of other less interesting things. Daylight, blue, radiant, filled the room with intense clarity, drawing luminous reflections from the varnished furniture, warming the heat of the tropics. A derelict butterfly, like a flower of the air, came in the balcony and rested on the roses of a very large vase. One rose lost some petals under its wings. Its petals fell like a perfumed weeping.

Fernando came in with a magnificent box of bonbons.

"From Marta, for you, with warm regards."

"Very thoughtful. How is she?"

"Embroidering a cape, with other ladies, for the Parish Virgin. They're her pastimes, the way she amuses herself. She's not like you, Natalia."

"A country flower, as you call her."

"When are you two getting married?" asked Sandoval.

Fernando seemed to think for a moment:

"This is April, isn't it...? One of these days, around the first part of December."

"December?..."

"Yes, December. Why?"

Natalia exclaimed:

"It's just that..."

The butterfly fluttering around the room landed on her shoulder, flapped its wings for an instant, and then flew away, gold and black...

"What, woman?"

"An old myth, a backwoods superstition..."

Seeing her hesitate, Fernando urged her on:

"Tell it, tell it...!"

"Well, they say that when a family celebrates two marriages in the same year, one of them will turn out to be a disaster."

"And that's what the two of you believe?"

"Not me; Sandoval."

Sandoval protested:

"No. That's not what I believe."

Whether they believed it or not, Fernando was getting married in December. He had arranged everything for then. The house, which was a rose-colored nest, lost in a garden where roses made up lattices and garlands. But what a nest, an altar. An altar dressed and perfumed for love. They would see then what a nest! Then they would see what an altar!

Don Lino came in, loudly giving orders to his manager:

"Tell those people not to act like fools. Tell them to go back to work, that nothing is happening."

Fernando asked:

"What's going on, Papa?"

"The men working the grounds have run off, and they've gone into hiding in the mountains: they're afraid of the war. Someone has gotten them to believe God knows what pack of lies. What they're trying to do is ruin the harvest."

"But the war is in Russia right now," put in Sandoval.

"That's like telling them it's in Peru," the manager groaned. "They're dead-set on believing that the Japanese are coming. And that they're not going to leave a stone standing."

A damn fairy-tale. For the first time in his life, Don Lino seemed to lose his dispassionate, passive temperament. Whether the Japanese came or not, what did it matter? Was the universe going to go unhinged because of that? Was that going to wipe the Philippines off the map? What did they think the Japanese were? The most humane of men; the most disciplined army; the best people in the world!

And slumping down despondently in an armchair, past the silence that his words caused, he conjured up the green cedars, fragrant branches; the paper house, the brightly colored lantern burning eternally for his life, the constant, enchanted little light that was waiting for him, glowing day and night...

Poor Haruko San! The sweet, eternally sweet "musme" that he had left silently weeping on the carpet, her arms open like two wounded wings that wished to fly, unable to fly after him, her forehead furrowed with pain above her poor, broken heart...!

V

It seemed strange to Don Lino, as he took his usual morning stroll, not to see the gardeners working. Later on they showed up, dressed very nicely, hat in hand, serious and formal...

"Ohayo."[36]

"What's happening? Where are you going?"

To Japan, sir. They were going back to their country. Important matters back home.

They were very sorry to have to leave the garden, the house, in such a hurry, but they had come to beg his pardon and to say goodbye. Their country, their home and their family came before anything else. If the men of their race could cry, by crying they would show him their deep regret.

Don Lino was annoyed. Now who would take care of that huge orchard that was his pride and joy? Who would trim that tree, making it willowy, making it lovely, and turn the bulb of the gladiola into a spray of flowers, into a bouquet of colorful butterflies?

Something unexpected, something traumatic and terrible was being hatched over the sea when these people were starting to go back to their country. Because it wasn't just Kenjiro and Otta. Don Lino was aware of an unusual exodus of a great number of Nipponese lately.

Things were not looking good. They seemed to be too clear-cut or too dark. Could the alarmists be right? Would future actions vindicate the war worries of his brother Ramon and so many more Filipinos who were drawing on a cruel pessimism regarding the nation's future?

Oh, that brother of his: so stern and severe in body and spirit, so opposite him in ideals and in ideas, antagonistic to pleasure, indifferent to women, dry and cold like a tree without branches and without nests.

He could just see him showing up suddenly, so that he could laugh at him and nettle him:

"What did I tell you? What did I warn you about, you big simpleton, you utter chump. Can you hear the gunshots, or are they raining down roses?"

He was aware of Japan's power, so enormous that, with all the poverty of its people, it invested three-fourths of its revenue into maintaining a huge fleet and a great army, both for offense and for defense. They sacrificed affectation and luxuries for it. For it, each Japanese was just a tiny river lost in the wide ocean of the Empire. The glory of the Mikado above all. And the greatness of the nation, without limits or horizons, from its distant ancestor, when Yeyasu[37] became manifest, the formidable "shogun" of the Tukegawa dynasty, the invincible warrior and profound philosopher, author of the immortal Decalogue.

He recalled the exquisite axioms...

"Perseverance is the foundation of eternal happiness." "The man who sees only the pinnacle of the plains and is ignorant of its sorrows, cannot call himself a man." "Life is a heavy bundle; if it flays your back you should not complain." "Anyone who allows himself to become intoxicated with human vanity is a fool." "Only we ourselves should be held accountable for our misfortunes." "All excess brings pain; a need for abundance is preferable"...

Each of these maxims was affixed to every Japanese spirit like a divine butterfly with a golden pin.

This was the keystone of its national grandeur; the philosophy of stress and pain; a disdain for life and for death; the radiant chimera of a people of poets in which the Sovereigns, dressed like European Generals, write in Asian characters glowing verses to spring; and the Empresses, since they are princesses, moan while plucking the "shamisen,"[38] sweet hymns to the cherry plum and to the pale moon.

The old man looked out sadly at his garden, festooned and redolent on this April day. He could picture it at the end of a few months, withered and desolate. The floriculturist magicians had gone away, and now no one would know how to wrest from the earth the secret of its verdant pomp, the miracle of the leaves like emeralds and the flowers like blue topaz, like fiery rubies, like purple amethyst.

He thought about our own people, the gardeners of the country, but immediately he dismissed the idea. They were a bunch of know-nothings, barbarians, with no notions of art or the finesse of an artist. They were all right for planting lettuce and cultivating tomatoes. But none of them knew the slightest thing about floriculture. In the Philippines, the land of flowers, the dandies bedecked themselves with cloth carnations; the women sought out perfume in bottles of eau de cologne imported from Paris, disdaining the jasmine necklace that freshened the grandmother's bosom; and in the few stately residences that rose above vast gardens, the flora appeared scanty, withered, abandoned.

At dinnertime he could barely eat a thing. He felt more anxious and dispirited than ever. His heart seemed to be warning him of a terribly painful future. Ponderously, he closed himself off in his room and stretched out on the bed. The hour for the Philippine siesta was beginning. Moving over the arc of the heavens, the sun rolled on toward the sea, burning red. One solitary songbird was warbling from the top of an acacia.

From the sea, through the garden foliage, came a brusque, warm breeze that rustled the pages of an illustrated magazine that Don Lino was using to summon sleep. From a piece of furniture came the silvery chiming of a musical clock. A minute went by, then several more minutes. The magazine slipped off the bed. And sleep spread its cloak of colors over the old man's eyelids...

All the Philippines had suddenly turned into a gigantic kuruma,[39] being pulled by our statesmen and guided by Japanese soldiers. They were marching over an infinite space that comprised all of Asia, and they were jogging along with such feverish enthusiasm that one would think they had been born for this, for bestial labor. The Japanese were pointing the way. And they were urging them on, with words full of hypocritical and deceitful politeness, to run wildly across the ground.

"What's happened to make these men act in such a degrading way as this?" he asked the first passer-by he came across. "Have they been rounded up and forced to do this?"

The stranger shrugged:

"Take a look at the armband with Japanese characters that they're flaunting so proudly. Read it..."

And Don Lino read:

VOLUNTEERS TO PULL THE KURUMA.

A fit of coughing woke him up. Pale and perspiring, he sat up in bed. Standing before him was Fernando, watching him affectionately:

"Lord, what a dream!"

"Indigestion?"

"An absurd nightmare."

They brought him a cup of tea, and he sipped it slowly. And along with the tea there was a file-folder full of papers that the gardeners, in their hasty departure, had left behind in their room.

"Was there something you wanted to tell me?"

Fernando looked at the bed, and as if he attached no importance to his words, he said simply:

"This morning I joined the Army."

The old man gave a start. What? Say that again. He hadn't heard that right...!

Fernando repeated his words:

"This morning I joined the Army."

There was a long, painful pause that Don Lino finally broke by putting his head in his hands:

"Why did you do that? What drove you to do that, and to make matters worse, without even consulting me?"

Fernando explained.

He considered it his duty. Everyone was doing it. From the youngest to the oldest men. There had been a call to action, and a widespread response. He wasn't going to spare his body when everyone else was going to the aid of the country.

"But you know what that means, what might happen?"

"That's why I joined."

Don Lino's anger flared up:

"And why do you have to fight against anybody, least of all against people who aren't our enemy, who have done nothing to us. And if they do come, they won't come against us?"

Oh, no! You go right back tomorrow morning to wherever it was, and take back your application. You don't have to get yourself killed for anyone's sake! You're not going to shoot any Japanese!

Fernando stepped back, visibly startled:

"But, Papa..."

"I beg you, I order you, I demand it!"

Impossible, it was over and done, he had taken the step, and above all he felt he was a man, and felt that he was a Filipino. A Filipino through and through, like Kalipulako,[40] Lakandula,[41] Sikatuna,[42] Solimán,[43] doing battle and fighting against the first conquerors, those horsemen from Iberia who came, dressed in iron, on their proud ships, to the beaches of Luzón and Visayas ...

From very far off, by Destiny and the designs of heaven, they came to see us over the green paths of the ocean. And powerful they were; concealing their chains of gold behind garlands of flowers, they bound our hands. Chains of gold, but in the end, chains! Then we lost the best of what God had given to us: our freedom! And from that time on, we stood watch, night and day, making amends and waiting for the moment when we could break apart those shackles. It was for that reason that the poet fell, singing before his death.[44] And Bonifacio,[45] crying out for independence. And Mabini,[46] writing the Decalogue of our sacred laws. And Luna,[47] with his sword in shatters... So they were, and so all we Filipinos should be. Those who do not feel or think that way, those who turn their backs on so much glory and so much sacrifice, who try to trade off or endanger a liberty that has cost us so much pain and so much blood, ought not call themselves Filipinos.

Don Lino stood up, proud and magnificent, his head erect and his arms open wide, as if he wanted to embrace all space:

"Very well, not another word. Make them kill you, commit suicide! For you, liberty is worth more than your father! And America is more important to you than Marta!"

Fernando sighed.

"She approves of what I'm doing."

"Then she doesn't love you."

He angrily protested this unjust affront:

"It's because she loves me with all her heart!"

They were silent, looking at each other furtively, warily, both of them afraid to continue talking, to continue stabbing each other in the heart with words. Until finally, Fernando suddenly felt his father's hands on his shoulders, and heard his voice tearfully saying:

"No matter what, I'm proud of you. You are so brave!"

Above the downcast face of Don Lino, Fernando's eyes fell upon the large crucifix hanging at the head of the bed. It kept watch over his dreams and presided over his sleepless nights. It was an ivory Christ, a true piece of antique art, an invitation to fall on one's knees and pray. Divine Lord! Why was He on the cross? Why had He shed His holy blood on the heads of the sons of Cain? They knew nothing of love, nor did they want to know! They only lived to hate and to commit crime! Their dogma was force and brutality. They destroyed cities by hurling down fire from the celestial vault created for the glow of stars. They sowed destruction upon the earth that formed the first man, the first sprout, the first flower. Fiercer than the beasts in the ocean, they turned its white spume into a red shroud, and its deep blue into an immense tomb. And since they could not crucify the Son again, because He was God, unattainable and glorious, they raised an enormous cross, a cross of burning iron, up to the highest point of the world and of life, in order to crucify Humanity!

A waft of wind pushed the file-folder of the Japanese men onto the floor, opening it and spilling out its papers. Fernando bent down to pick them up, examining them and reading them surreptitiously. Suddenly he frowned, and his lips drew back in a bitter smile...

"Take a look at this, Papa."

Don Lino picked up the pages and began to examine them himself.

In his service he'd employed, as his gardeners, a pair of distinguished men. Because Otta turned out to be a captain in the Japanese navy.

And Kenjiro, a commander of the imperial armed forces...

American and Filipino troops surrendering at Bataan, Luzon, Philippines, 9 Apr 1942
Source: United States National Parks Service
Retrieved from: https://ww2db.com/image.php?image_id=4247

PART II

I

All the newspapers came out, announcing Germany's great victories. Half of Europe lay crushed at its feet. The other nations began to look at it in horror. These had tragically fallen: France, Belgium, Holland, Austria, Greece, Yugoslavia, Czechoslovakia, Poland, Norway, Denmark, Luxembourg, Albania, and the Baltic States: Estonia, Lithuania, Latvia...

Now they were heading to Russia, to conquer Leningrad and Moscow. The forces of the Fuehrer were taking on the reputation of being invincible. And Hitler[48] was marching forward, thinking he would march the way Alexander had, and the Roman Caesars and Napoleon, while there were still worlds to conquer. "Deutschland über alles."[49]

An Asiatic empire, ambitious, cunning and aggressive, peered at itself in this mirror with its tiny eyes, armed to the teeth. Why couldn't it be the Germany of the Orient? Why not drag the war over to the Pacific, where it would be so easy to carry out the same criminal actions as the Nazis? Who would be able to bridle them in? Who would be able to trample them underfoot?

In the river of blood that Hitler had stirred up, Japan, a league of fishermen, could make a fine catch. It was a matter of closing your eyes and leaping boldly into the adventure of combat. Who said anything about fear? Set sail over the water! If the fishing was good, the great Asia, dreamed of so often, would rise above it, dominant and magnificent. If an ill wind capsized the vessel, there still remained the towering harakiri,[50] like a golden brooch, to draw its history to a close..

Treacherously, the spying services began to intensify. And they began to put into play their two-faced diplomacy. Where was the main enemy? America? America didn't want war, and it wasn't prepared for war. So then, the moment, the great psychological and yearned-for moment had arrived to strike the crushing blow. There would be no lack of pretexts or reasons.

Under such circumstances, the Axis powers showed themselves to be more egotistical and audacious than ever, while their people were bathing in an abundance of rose water. The Germans and Italians of Manila were beginning to look down their noses at all other mortals. They were calling themselves the best men in the world, the chosen ones, the only sons of God. In the meanwhile, America was sleeping, dreaming of a quick peace. And the Philippines, naïve and happy, dressed for a festival, were singing and dancing.

They were singing and dancing upon a burning crater, despite the alarm that was rapidly spreading across the editorials in the newspapers, and in military and official circles. It is so difficult to accept the premise that at any given moment we will pass from sublime happiness and well-being into an inferno of horror and devastation!

To certify the indifference to the catastrophe, Professor Anselmi, his back to the piano, brazenly and arrogantly proposed marriage to Robles' daughter. From the very first day she had captivated him. He dreamed of her and was consumed with passion. Her image was always before his eyes, her voice in his ears, her perfume in his soul. Oh, if only she loved him! If she shared his wildly romantic dreams!

Before the trembling Natalia, who was pale with indignation and astonishment, Anselmi opened the golden leaves of a fan with a magical landscape. Voyages, festivals, artistic triumphs, a honeymoon with no clouds or waning. She, like a queen, and the entire world an enchanted palace for her. And he, always at her side, the leading knight of her court, the eternal troubadour of her kingdom, always faithful and loving, rendering homage to her.

This unexpected, sudden and fantastic proposal ended up shaking Natalia, so naturally nervous and haughty, to her very core. Although her stupor lasted only a moment. She exploded with a dry, cutting voice, staring at the musician:

"You jerk!"

He? Why? Someone as important as he was? Why? For laying a divine passion and future at her feet?

"Jerk...! Clown...!

As though by magic, Sandoval arrived unexpectedly. Natalia grabbed hold of his arm the way a warrior would hold tight his shield.

"Throw that man out of here!"

Not understanding, Sandoval hesitated. Then she picked up her purse and took out a wad of bills that she threw at Anselmi:

"Here's what you want, what you came looking for...!

"Porca miseria! Miserable vita!"

In the blink of an eye, quietly, ignominiously, the professor disappeared from view. She slumped into a chair, ripping up her fragrant handkerchief with her teeth and fingernails...

"Jerk...! Clown...!"

She blamed herself for the insolence because she had always been so good-natured and friendly with him. What was that guy thinking? That she was made of the same muck as other women, the ones who hitched their star to the first foreign ignoramus they met just because their skin was lighter, and they could mince and flaunt their voice, singing Rigoletto.[51]

Faced with Natalia's explosion of hysterics, Sandoval called to mind his diplomas from three distinguished universities, and thought of himself as a physician as well as a loving protector. He found tranquilizers; he gave her medicine; and when he saw that she had finally calmed down, he intoned an epic hymn to his prowess.

That's the way women should be; all our women. No respect or concern for certain entities who think they belong to a superior race, and who take women to be abandoned fields and open cities. What sort of true passion could they feel for them? What sort of fantasy, with them being so different in blood and in their customs? They were only looking out for riches. The most beautiful girls, if they were poor, weren't worthy of the slightest bit of wooing by these moneygrubbers. They aimed for the pocketbook. And once they had the pocketbook packed and at their disposal, then they saved their real caresses and amorous feelings for the females of their race, at the price of gold for a minute of love.

Dukes, Marquises, Counts! Almost all of them the sons of great, blue-blooded families. Some of them even swore that in their lineage they were direct descendants of Charlemagne himself! The truth was that they had come to this country, poor and dirty, with tattered shoes, carrying a bundle of clothes on their back.

But since this was the land of incredible metamorphoses, and inexplicable and absurd aggrandizements, these swindlers were sprouting up day and night, dressed and treated like princes at the highest levels of our society. And take your illustrious descendant of Duke So-and-So, and the Marquis of Such-and-Such! The sad consequences of Philippine candor were felt very late, when some poor girl, robbed and abandoned, fell from the tall tower of her fantasies to bathe, in tears of despair, the little fair-haired heads of a couple of hungry, threadbare, petite half-castes who were crying for their father, asking for something to eat.

He had traveled a great deal through towns where parasites like those came from. He knew them well. He knew of some who had been sentenced to penitentiaries in America and Europe; some who had abandoned their women and their families to go wandering around the world like wolves, stalking victims to slaughter in order to better themselves and their fortunes. And in the Philippines, like no other corner of the world, they found opportune victims in the innocent, trusting man who let himself be dazzled by their flashy lies, and in the romantic and gullible woman who lent an ear to their fallacious amorous serenatas.

As Sandoval talked, he walked back and forth, gesturing, bombastic, in circles around his fiancée who was still furious. She didn't hear him, she couldn't understand him. She was thinking about the musician, about how nervy he was, about his cynicism, with an urge and vehement desire for revenge. Why had she held back? Why hadn't she slapped his face...?

"Why didn't you tell him off...? Why didn't you give him a beating...?"

Sandoval melted with excuses:

"I didn't know... I didn't understand... I'd just come in..."

Natalia thundered out:

"Well, you should have understood, man! He tried to seduce me, to stab you in the back like a traitor; he insulted us all...!"

"Well, if you want, I'll go right out, and find him and clobber him."

A servant came in, and announced that someone was on the phone, calling for the doctor.

"Excuse me. It must be one of my very distinguished patients..."

He went to the telephone in a hallway in the house, far away from where Natalia was pounding her slender, nervous feet on the magnificent carpet that stretched all along the room.

"Doctor Sandoval speaking. Who is calling?"

"Signore Bruno Anselmi, Count de Blardoni."

He shuddered with a shock of outrage, grasping the receiver like a club:

"What Count, and what pigs that fly! What you are is nothing but a monstrous snake in the grass!"

This did not bring any change to the professor's beautiful voice:

"Ma, I'm calling you to challenge you to a gentlemen's duel, not for you to insult me. I have been crudely humiliated in your presence by a signorina that you must answer for. I cannot challenge the signorina. I challenge you."

"Whenever and wherever you want, right now..."

"Right now, no; that's impossible. Ma, tonight, at exactly twelve o'clock, I'll be waiting for you with my witnesses, at the bandstand of the Luneta..."

And he hung up.

That music box from hell! He was going to beat the crap out of him! He was going to blow his brains out! Him and the whole gang of flute players that came with him...!

That night, alone and armed with a small "Colt," Sandoval walked over to where they were supposed to meet. No one there. Not a soul all along the footbath. The sound of the sea close by. The quivering of the stars in the dense shadows. And rising from the sea and the night like a branch of lights and flaming sparklers, Cavite,[52] a little further off...

From time to time he took a look at his wristwatch. He had spent the whole blessed night keeping watch over the stars. Full of anger and bitterness, he drew his revolver and aimed at the bandstand. Several shots rang out in the day's beautiful dawning...

Bang!
"For the musicians!"
Bang!
"For divine art!"
Bang! Bang!
"For the mother who gave birth to the music staff!"

II

Doctor Kauffman had just sterilized the syringe he used to give Don Lino a shot for his bronchitis, and he sat down heavily in an armchair.

"All the rushing about is over now. Now we can spend our time talking; this morning I closed my clinic; you're going to have to find a new doctor..."

In the living room, in addition to Don Lino, were Don Ramon and Father Elías, the sixtyish priest who presided over the church on the Robles estate. A righteous and learned man, devoted to sowing goodness. He had the reputation among his parishioners of being virtuous, and of dividing his time between religious duties and his deep affection for everything that was small and weak: children, birds, vagrants.

Kauffman continued talking:

"I'm getting my things in order; making a will, Lino. Inside of a month, perhaps sooner, they'll have all us Axis nationals in prison."

Don Lino showed his distress:

"What can I do for you?"

"Right now, offer me a glass of beer."

They brought in bottles of ice-cold beer, club soda, and a bottle full of amber-colored alcohol: whiskey. Who was the whiskey for? Terribly intoxicating, according to the German doctor. They needed to drink beer, the liquid gold of the Rhine, the giver of health and strength. Its essence nourished the body the same way the fairy tales of the Black Forest fed the spirit. You had to laugh at the miserable champagne of France and the rest of the alcoholic concoctions of other countries. Nothing like beer, light and dark, like the musical keystone that inspired a god named Wagner.[53] Dark froth and flaxen froth, braids of dawn and night of mermaids that two lyrical princes, Goethe[54] and Heine,[55] unbound with their fingers thirsting for glory.

He raised his glass brimming with golden bubbles.

"Prosit!"

Don Lino imitated him:

"Salud!"

And Kauffman continued spouting:

"Germany has to win the war. Hitler is an instrument of divine providence. Everything that's happening to democratic nations, because of their scandalous debauchery, is a punishment from the Creator!"

Don Ramon let out a loud laugh. Father Elías stood up, protesting:

"Don't say that, Mr. Doctor! As a priest, I cannot allow it! The crimes that men commit, the wars that destroy nations, are the natural and logical result of their own wickedness, their lack of religion, and their arrogance. God does not punish. God forgives! God is love, goodness, mercy. If not, with Him being able to demolish the world with just one word, why did He let Himself be crucified, and in His horrible agony promise Paradise to the thief who was dying at His side and who asked Him for salvation?"

"Pious yarns, Father!"

"Are you Catholic?"

"I have my own religion."

Don Ramon chipped in:

"The religion of Germany: 'Deutschland über alles.'"

The German spun around:

"In science, in art, in culture, in everything!"

"With a hail of cannon fire!"

"Don't be that way, Ramon. What do you leave for the ignorant, for the poor in spirit by spouting such monstrosities?"

Don Ramon sat up in his seat:

"Thanks for that business about the poor in spirit and the ignorant, but I want to tell you something, Fritz, and you can take it any way you want to. I respect your loyalty to your country, but I don't give a damn for your political ideas. And everything you rant about democracies goes in one ear and out the other... No, don't lose patience; let me go on... Germany could be a great country, just the way Italy could; but both of them without a clown of a schoolteacher who's turned himself into a Duce, without that raging anti-Semitic madman, Hitler, and without the disgraceful, pestilent alliance with so many millions of Japanese "kurumeros"[56] disguised as imperial troops. Sometimes force can overrule, but it never prevails. Some might bend a knee to Parsifal.[57] But in the face of Nazi cannons, you can't feel anything but horror and hatred."

Kauffman shrugged:

"If our cannons bellow out, it's because they've been provoked. When Germany goes to war, it's not because it enjoys causing harm. It goes like a surgeon with a red-hot iron to heal a dangerous, disgusting wound!"

"A damn lie! You've never healed anything. With your course of action, the only thing you've done is win countless battles! And what does that mean...?"

"Doesn't it mean anything?".

"Nothing! Because in the end, you've lost, and you'll continue to lose, all the wars!"

In one swallow, Kauffman drank all the beer left in his glass. And he had them bring him another. It was better to drink. Why go on arguing with somebody who didn't have a clue?

"The day the Nips come here to bombard this place, you can go out on the street without a care. You are so hard-headed, Ramon, that there's no bomb capable of punching its way through it. I give you my word as a doctor. I guarantee it."

The gong rang, announcing mealtime, and they all went into the dining room. They were staying to eat. Natalia, Fernando and Sandoval showed up shortly afterward.

"Now the family's complete!" remarked Don Lino. Because it was as though Sandoval, Kauffman and Father Elías were all part of the Robles family.

On the table, covered with an immaculate tablecloth, overflowing with silver and glassware, there came the soft perfume of roses, the sweet, pungent smell of bananas, pineapples and mangos. Beautiful fruit of the Philippine sun, with the aroma of a flower and the distinctive taste of honey.

"I'll begin with this, the mango and the pineapple. They're loaded with vitamins. And besides that, they taste like heaven."

They were serving oysters seasoned with lemon juice and pepper; magnificent king shrimp and crabs drowning in thick, redolent sauces; roasted turkey with strawberry gel; pie with poultry giblets...

"A feast for an Archbishop, Father Elías," grumbled Kauffman with his mouth full; it was astonishing how these lordly Agric. nabobs treat themselves...!

When it was time for dessert, while the coffee was steaming from the tiny cups and the green, red and amber liquors could be seen in the thin goblets, Sandoval, sitting up in his chair, announced haughtily, as if this was a national event, that he was joining the Medical Corps of the Army. He didn't want to be less worthy than all those other members of his profession who were walking out on the streets in their uniforms. He had always made fun of the famous lieutenants. But now the circumstances were demanding it. And he was one more lieutenant.

His words were received with an indifferent silence that Natalia finally broke, applauding the future hero with her small hands. But Don Lino smiled mockingly, trying to take him down a peg:

"Are there a lot of your companions strolling around out there, showing off their panache?"

"Forty, fifty, maybe more..."

"Well then, the sick people are in luck."

Sandoval turned red:

"Why do you say that?"

"Oh, my friend! Because of the undertakers! The days of colossal business rates are over!"

Although if they imagined they were going to kill the Japanese the same way they killed their own patients, they were cheeky bastards!...

"I'm not talking about you! Don't take it the wrong way."

Kauffman laughed and laughed, and when he was tired of laughing, he began to talk very seriously:

"Don't you folks get offended by what I'm going to suggest. I've been in this country for so long and I care for you so much, that I almost feel more like I'm a Filipino than a German. I want to tell you that this land was created for love, not for war. This is a nation made to live, not to rise up or fall down killing or dying. Here children grow up tied to their mother's apron strings, and they are taught only to pray and sing until they are nice and big, and then they are sent off to school. In other countries, the boys turn into soldiers the moment they come out of the womb, and when they begin to play, they play at war with cardboard soldiers, with sticks for guns and with tin swords. The warrior spirit and love for the military is pounded into them almost before they learn how to babble their first words, or can stand up and walk without the help of nursemaids or walkers. They're treated like men when they're still children. They're given more physical training than an education in morals. And all this takes place especially in Germany and, as a matter of fact, in Japan too."

I still remember, as if it were yesterday, the sound advice of my father before he sent me off to the university: Fritz, my boy, you're fifteen years old now, and you have to start being a man. In order to live, to succeed, to come out ahead, you have to be strong, you need to have courage. Don't ever act like a coward or be afraid of anyone or anything. Hammer your way through life. Life is a wicked old lady who despises and destroys cowards, and offers up all its gifts and caresses to the ones who are able to put their foot on its neck. Instead of listening to what's in your heart, listen to what reason has to say. And remember always, that on land and on sea and in space, the smallest things are devoured by the biggest ones. Try to be an eagle in the wind, a shark in the ocean, a leopard among men.

Don Lino nodded his head approvingly at everything the German said. When that man was silent, he began to take the floor:

"Here, Mama and Papa make sure their little boys don't get 'boo-boos,' so they always try to keep them with nice little older girls, playing dolls or jump rope. Nothing to do with the dirt or the sun. No rough and tumble, or snooty attitudes. They're washed, perfumed and dressed up with great care every day. And every night we set their hair on end with tales about witches, ghosts and goblins. And at the first naughty thing they do, there's the threat of a boogeyman who snatches away children and eats them raw. When a little boy has a fight outside with another boy, and comes back with a black eye or a torn shirt, instead of congratulating him and cheering on his spunk, he's given a stiff spanking. 'You won't ever settle things with your fists,' he's warned. 'That's for little boys in the streets, for low-class people, the children of good-for-nothings. Well behaved children, good children don't do that. If any of your schoolmates gives you trouble, you go and tell the teacher; the teacher will take care of it. Don't try to settle it yourself.'"

These children grow up, and when they're ten years old they smoke, at fifteen they start to make love with women; and when they're twenty or thirty, when they think they're men because they've finished their academic studies or they're beginning to grow whiskers, they turn out to be a physically and morally ridiculous lot, a bunch of absolute sissies. You're right, great Doctor! Our land isn't a land for heroic deeds. On our anvil we don't forge soldiers. The day some powerful enemy comes to invade us, they'll just waltz right in and have their own way...

"Just a minute, Lino...!" shouted Don Ramon.

But Fernando's nervous, rising voice exploded:

"Here, in the absence of better forces, whoever comes, whenever they come, if they come, they'll run into the living wall of our heart. Maybe it will turn out to be weak and will crumble before the impact of an enemy who is more powerful and greater in numbers.[51] But that doesn't mean that we are unmanly or cowards in any way. It only means that there are few of us and that our mothers didn't give birth to us so that we'd turn out to be criminals or hoodlums. I've been the sort of child that you just described, Papa. For a while I lived in that beautiful country of giants and dwarfs. Little Red Riding Hood was my companion. And the prince who wandered around, searching for love with a little shoe, like a glass flower in his hands, was, for me, the greatest of men. I don't know, I've never known how to fight or hurt anyone. I would never make trouble. But I swear to you that the day I saw the first Filipino fall, attacked by a foreign invader, I couldn't be held accountable for the way I'd act. Because it's one thing to be peaceful, and it's something else to be a coward. And I think all other Filipinos feel the same way I do."

"You are a Robles. Your grandfather was a Spaniard," exclaimed Don Lino. "You have a lot of Quijote[58] in your blood..."

Kauffman, smiling and red as a pepper, turned to Father Elías:

"And what do you say, Father?"

Father Elías lifted his head.

"What would you have me say, Mr. Doctor? The Divine Master says: All those who live by the sword, will perish by the sword."

III

That afternoon Fernando put on his uniform for the first time. And he didn't recognize himself.

He saw another man in front of the mirror, another Fernando, taller, prouder, more distinguished. Look at what clothes can do! The transition made by an outfit loaded with flashy stripes and gold badges. Marta was sure to look at him with eyes filled with a glittering illusion.

"How do I look, Papa?"

Don Lino let the newspaper he was reading fall at the unexpected sight of the smart-looking captain. And looking him over from head to toe, he asserted peevishly:

"For girls to fall in love with your looks, you'll suit them to a T. To let yourself be shot defending Americans, a whole lot better."

The eternal song of the old man, lacking in emotion as always.

As he was leaving, he found Natalia bent over a clump of jasmines, picking flowers, both hands full of flowers:

"How do I look, huh?"

Natalia stood up, blinking as though before a golden streak of lightning:

"Wonderful... You look like a prince... Like a general right out of Hollywood..."

Another man, yes, completely new and different from the Fernando of the sets of modernist ties, with a yellow rose, and a bright carnation in the button hole of a white jacket. Another person in body and especially in spirit since he found himself girthed by the khaki cuirass that seemed to imprison him in new dignity and new honor. Now he could call himself a Filipino through and through. Now he could feel like he was a true patriot. And even stand at attention before the Hero of the race, before all the country's heroes, to say to them reverently:

"We, we who salute the dawn, will not forget those who fell at night!"

He continued on his way to his fiancée's house in Santa Mesa.

And the same question when he stood before the sweet, pale fiancée:

"How do I look, Marta?"

But Marta did not reply. She could not speak, because she was crying.

A bad dream? That torment – a palpable overwhelming reality, that perpetual agitation of her heart for something inevitably cruel and painful that would upset her passion and her life. Here was the hero of her dreams, now wrapped in the toga of abnegation and sacrifice. She saw him for an instant, completely stained in blood and gold that was not the gold or purple of twilight at the dying of the day. And she embraced him, shattered, sobbing...

"Nando... Nando..."

Like a child, like a treasure, like a bouquet of heavenly flowers, he held her in his arms...

Why shed tears like this? Why moan about something that wasn't worth making her pretty eyes sad? What had she found in him to make her grieve so much? Did she find him so repulsive that he had frightened her to tears? Marta, for heaven's sake!

Little by little, she grew calmer, wiping away teardrops like a sky full of rain drops after a storm. Clothed by a sky of blue, her eyes shone like stars over the blue. After this passing painful crisis, all that remained were sighs...

"Excuse me, I was being foolish. I couldn't help myself. I love you so much!..."

"But, woman..."

"Yes, you said it... Woman. I'm jealous of the country."

With his lips he gathered the last tear that was clouding her eyes. Even her tears were sweet and fragrant! Even her tears...!

He lulled her like an innocent, wounded turtledove:

"Nothing can compare with your fine, smooth face, a pale half-moon under the night of your flowing hair. Nothing like your eyes that illuminate, with the holy light of sanctuaries, the things that they reflect. Nothing comparable to your mouth, a nest of pearls and rose petals for the goldfinch of your voice, for the skylark of your laughter. Nothing like your hands with their feather-like caresses. Nothing like your feet, butterflies so light that they must be kissed slowly so that they do not break when they are kissed. And nothing like the rhythm of your body, like slow music, taking wing as you walk..."

Later, more calm, she began showing him the large boxes full of nuptial finery prepared by the couturiers. It was a world full of tulle, chiffon and lace.

This was the wedding dress, immaculate, a white, silk cocoon where the chrysalis would throb tremulously before becoming a flower of wings and colors. This was the veil, a long, perfumed cloud that she would trail like a queen, to the altar of the holy Sacrament. And these, the rest of the clothing, of every style and shade. And the undergarments, fine and embroidered, covered with ribbons, lace and other strips of cloth. And the other little shoes and slippers made of satin and silver and gold thread...

"Look at that negligee," she said, blushing, "and tell me if you don't think it's like the gown of a fairy..."

"Of your fairy godmother."

"And at this dress that's like a dream..."

A woman, in the end, in love and young, excited, while looking at her gorgeous, new wardrobe, like a child with his favorite toys. She went along folding and unfolding clothes, displaying them like banners of her fantasy. All that would help make her beautiful, wrap her in waves of beauty and fragrance when she would need more than ever, outside of love in body and soul, to be beautiful and fair.

There remained only sixty days until they were to be married. She spent them just like the beads of a giant rosary of passion, praying their mysteries of pain and joy and glory. Together, they had already chosen the cottage where they would live, a small one, where they would live united forever, so they would always be in sight of one another, at every moment, where they would even be able to hear each other breathe. And they had agreed on everything they bought: from the most luxurious furniture, to the tableware and the crystal ware.

They dreamed of a future life of poets. And in this ardent, soaring fantasy, with wings of fire and talons of gold, they lifted into the air the castle of Romeo and Juliet, the silk ladder, the madrigal under the moon.

And among the jasmines that awoke, rustling their flowers, and the stars that went to sleep at the awakening of the jasmines, Marta's voice always, always, always...

"Don't leave my arms, my love. It is not yet dawn. The lark has not yet sung."

Don Eladio congratulated Fernando enthusiastically. He was carrying out his duty, and that was very good. The uniform he was wearing now, just like so many thousands of young Filipinos, was the best argument in favor of our cause. Ah, if he, Gala, had ten fewer years on his back. He would certainly be there with his rifle on his shoulder, ready to shoot the morning star.

Of course, for the women, for Marta especially, so sensitive and so much in love, the thought of mortal danger would turn into an outpouring of wailing and moans. The woman in love is selfish, whether she is a mother, a wife, a lover. She has nothing but her love. She has no fear other than losing her beloved. That was why they weren't surprised to notice Marta crying. Also hearing her cry and guessing the reason for it, her mother had wept silently in a corner. Women's things. Sentimentality and romantic ideas that turned into tears. Clouds, grey clouds over the brightness of our life. Water that the wind pushed forward, turned to rain, mist, tears...

When Fernando said goodbye to his beloved, she smiled happily, once again hopeful, her past anguish completely forgotten. With words of optimism and persuasion, he had convinced her of how absurd it was to get upset over bad things that would never come to pass. And it was not difficult to cover the eyes of spring with a scarf of flowers so that they would not be able to contemplate pain. And it is so easy to chase away the sad fears of a woman in love, with kisses and tender murmurs!

On the way back to his house, Fernando felt thirsty: it was a thirst that seemed to come from a feverish state that was melancholically searing his heart. He drove his car to a Night Club. He needed to drink, get drunk on music and alcohol, feel the bustle of happy, carefree people, get light-headed...

The dance hall was teeming with life. Dozens of couples were dancing frenetically to the sounds of a brass band. He sat down at a small table that was miraculously free. At another table, large and full of wineglasses, tumblers and purses and fans, a group of women and men in formal dress were enjoying themselves.

He suddenly noticed that they had their eyes on him:

"Who is that?" he heard a female voice ask.

And another voice replied loudly:

"Robles, woman! Fernando Robles, the son of the millionaire..."

Without looking at anyone, he felt all eyes fastened on him. And he called the waiter over:

"Bring me champagne."

He lit a cigarette and swept his eyes over the hall. At the corner table, they were still talking about him:

"Look at him, enlisting in the Army, stinking rich the way he is! Why would that man have joined the Army?"

"To show off his uniform, girl. They're more handsome in a uniform."

He was served the champagne, and the hapless figure of an old friend, the bohemian, the reporter Andrade appeared before him.

"Carlos, my good man, I'm so glad to see you, have a seat..."

Andrade turned excitedly:

"My dear Robles...! My very dear Fernando...! You here, and dressed like a supreme commander...! Am I dreaming...?"

They filled their drinks, they talked about trivial matters. And Fernando suddenly burst out with the question that had been gnawing at him for some time:

"Do you know those characters at that table?"

Andrade knew everyone. He was the society editor of "La Linterna." The women were the Pérez, the Santos and the Claraval. The men were the professional crème de la crème of the country, all of them with doctor's degrees. Gutiérrez, an M.D.; De la Cruz, a lawyer; Martínez, an optician; Peláez, a dentist; Melendres, a professor at the University of the Philippines; and Rocha, a veterinarian. The cream of the crop of society. To sum it all up, the men and the women, several thousand pesos of debts and trickery.

Fernando smiled.

"Are you interested in them? Have you fallen in love with that scarecrow of a Claraval? Do you want to dance with the best of the Pérez women, the one who looks like candied ham? They're the friendliest girls in the world. I'll introduce you to them, and in five minutes the whole group of doctors will be left beggared. You'll captivate them simply with your feet. All you have to do is take them, one at a time, to dance the tango."

Fernando continued to smile. Andrade kept dishing the dirt while he guzzled down champagne:

"These girls, and those over there, and the ones way over in the back, and all of them, all, all the ones who are here, for you and any man like you, easy as cake. If you want, I'll introduce you to them, altogether, and at four o'clock in the morning you'll be able to climb up on that platform there, or where those bloody musicians are murdering art, and shout out like Caesar: 'Veni, vidi, vici.'"[59]

Then, breaking off his cynical brassiness of a journalist, he found himself obliged to explain the reason for his interest in those people. They had been rude to him. They had nearly made his blood boil...

"They're probably drunk. I see their table full of bottles, and they don't know how to drink. As soon as they have a pint of beer in their craw, they think they're movie stars. But you get up, you go and take a swipe at the best of them, and they won't do a thing, my dear Robles!".

Look at the hope of the nation! Look at the young men! In the valiant prime of life! Those backwoods country girls and those ignorant farmhands are a whole lot more respectable!

After finishing his second drink, Fernando got up to leave. He had come to find refuge in society, and that society turned out to be crass, disagreeable. The pleasant music he was looking for was just a rumbling of mangled metal and shrill honking. The ice-cold wine to satisfy his thirst, instead of comforting him, had only made him light-headed, only increasing his unaccountable malaise.

"I'm leaving, Andrade."

"Goodbye, and congratulations. Tomorrow I'll print out your photograph and make a great ballyhoo about it in the newspaper."

"No, man. Please. I don't wear this uniform to brag or make myself out to be brave. I beg you, if you want to remain my friend, don't do such an awful thing."

He went out. On the road he kept thinking of Marta. It pained him to have misled her like a child, making her believe that the war was far away, when not he or anyone could be certain of that, and war might be nearer than anyone thought. Marta! How he loved her! What a bounty of love! What rapturous love he felt for that woman!

He remembered two years ago, when he had first declared his love, and she timidly protested because he compared her to the dove in the woods and the country flowers...

"Oh, no, Mr. Robles! I'm not a flower or a dove. I'm just Marta, at your service. But you are a poet, and you like to tell lies, the way all poets do. Once you even called me a cherub and compared me to the dawn. Oh, no sir! That's not the way to win me. The day you stop mixing me up with all the things I'm not, and call me precisely by my real name, maybe then I'll answer you the way you want, and satisfy your complaint..."

Now in his room, in his bed, praying dreamily and thinking of her as never before, he began to fall asleep with her sweet image under his closed eyelids, with the prayer abandoned between his half-open lips...

"...blessed are you among women..."

IV

B lessed are you among women..."

On her knees, her hands crossed over her breast and her face raised to the altar, Marta was praying at the feet of the Virgin.

She had already heard the first mass, because she had gone to the church of Santo Domingo very early, when the doors were first opened and the lights were on.

She spent a long while praying, asking for mercy, talking to the Virgin. She mixed prayers in with her pleas. She begged for love as she whispered the prayer of San Bernardino: "Remember, O most gracious Virgin Mary, that never was it known that anyone who implored thy help was left unaided."

It was the first day of October, and the temple seemed to be covered with adornments. The festival for Our Lady of the Rosary was beginning. Silver candelabra and gold bouquets were everywhere. Artistic folds of sumptuous damasks and embroidered velvets tumbled from high polychromatic windows down to the carpeted floor. The bronze lamps glowed from on high – enormous chandeliers of crystal and gold – sparkling like precious stones when they are touched by light. In the choir appeared the magical trumpets of the organ, ready to flood the arches and naves with harmony.

The smell of the temple was that of snuffed incense, or burnt candle wax, and of freshly opened flowers. An incessant murmur, the monotone of prayers, wafted like a faint stirring of bees. Marta very faintly heard her mother's voice:

"Shall we pray the Rosary?".

They began to recite it together, with Doña Claudia starting. There were fifty Ave Marias losing their petals before the altar, like fifty immaculate lilies used by the new angels to greet the Servant of God throughout the centuries, over all the lands.

The bells pealed, announcing new masses. The naves became filled with the faithful who were beginning to pour into the temple. It was starting to get warm. And the women's fans opened, fluttering like large paper butterflies.

Marta and her mother continued to pray:

"Regina sine labe originali concepta."

"Ora pro nobis."

"Regina Sacratissimi Rosarii."

"Ora pro nobis."

"Regina pacis."

"Ora pro nobis."

Suddenly and unexpectedly, it seemed to Natalia that someone was talking to her:

"Are you going to be here much longer?"

She shook her head, no.

"All right then. I'll wait for you. You can come with me and spend the day at my house."

Doña Claudia looked at Natalia, half smiling and half shocked. What a girl! Chattering away in church. It leads the way to temptation. And right in the middle of mass.

She humbly made the sign of the cross three times, to drive away the devil And she continued to pray the divine litany:

"Agnus Dei, qui tollis peccata mundi."

Marta responded:

"Parce nobis, Domine."

"Agnus Dei, qui tollis peccata mundi."

"Exaudi nos, Domini.

"Agnus Dei, qui tollis peccata mundi."

"Misere nobis..."

The Rosary finished, they stood up. The cars were waiting at the door of the church. Natalia took Marta with her, throwing kisses to Doña Claudia:

"You and Don Eladio come to pick her up tonight. Otherwise, she'll be gone forever; you'll never see her again..."

When Doña Claudia started to protest, they were already far, far away, in the brand-new "Lincoln" that seemed to have wings, flying to the Ermita. That Natalia was a handful. Wilier than a fox, she had snatched away her daughter just like a highly skilled lady's man could have.

In the meantime, at her house now, Natalia was pounding on her brother's door.

"Isn't today your birthday?"

From inside, without opening the door, Fernando answered:

"You're wrong, cupcake. The one who's celebrating today is your future pluperfect. Look at the Almanac. Saint Nicodemus, virgin and martyr."

"That's too bad, Fernando."

"Why?"

"Because I've brought you a wonderful gift."

There were footsteps. There was laughter. Unexpectedly, the door opened. And Fernando, speechless from emotion and surprise, found Marta before him, still wearing the veil from the mass, smelling like incense and prayers, a ray of blessed sunshine that the day greeted him with...

They spent hours barely apart from each other, the girls making music in the living room, Fernando reciting verses in the garden, amid the green rustling of the foliage and the shady canopy of orchids of one of the Japanese pagodas. In the evening Don Ramon and Sandoval arrived. And when they turned on the lights, Fernando unexpectedly found Marta alone and entranced in front of the large portrait of his mother.

"I look like her, don't I?"

"Much more than Natalia does."

"Natalia looks like Papa."

"She was very beautiful, Nando."

"She was very good."

"Do you remember what she was like?"

How could he forget her? It was like he could still see her now, like he could still hear her, like he still felt her in his heart and in his life.

"I was thirteen years old when she went away, and she gave me a perfect understanding of what love is, what pain is."

"Did she love you a lot? Did you love her very much?"

"The way you love me. The way I love you."

He pulled her close and put his head next to hers, and continued to talk while they both gazed at the portrait.

"My mother didn't seem like a woman. She seemed more like a faerie, Marta. She spoke and moved about without making any noise. Her body seemed to be full of light. Her soul was that of singing harps and fragrant spikenards.

When you met her, you would wonder why the wings sprouting from her shoulders were missing. And you would ask: How did this angel lose the gift of flight? And when you saw everything she did, you would be even more bewildered. Because her entire spirit was committed to loving. And her entire existence was given over to prayer and work.

That's the way my mother was, like good mothers of men are, and like all women who are mothers should be. From the lowest, Eve, to the highest, Mary. Both of them saints. Saints, all of them. The one who cries disconsolately when she loses paradise forever, the same as the one who reopens the door to paradise, kneeling at the foot of the cross, kissing the feet of the bloodied Son."

Marta shivered as she listened to the poet.

"And I'm talking to you this way, I dare to speak to you like this, despite all the abominable slanderers of women, because I am absolutely convinced that your son, our future son, will be certain to say the same things about you that I'm telling you about my mother."

"Oh..." she moaned, overwhelmed with modesty and honor.

He continued to talk, even more impassioned:

"What happens, Marta, is that men don't ever realize, or when they do, it's too late, what a mother means to all of them. Despite everything that has been written about this, or put into poetry, it almost always remains just words or poetry. In reality, there are very few men who know how to love and honor the woman who gave them life the way she should be honored and adored. That's why in every mother there is a martyr. And that's why she is a saint. Because it is pain that makes saints into saints. And because the roads that lead to God are roads full of thorns..."

Don Ramon interrupted them:

"Praying before your mother, eh? Blessed Margarita."

Fernando turned around:

"Did you want something, uncle?""

"I'm looking for your father, but don't bother, I know where I'll find him..."

He went to Don Lino's office and found him slumped in an armchair, his elbows on his writing table, his head sunk between his hands.

"Are you feeling sick?"

"I feel devastated."

Devastated? Why? Is it because you're starting to take what might happen seriously? Where had he left the bulging treasure chest of his unbridled optimism? Where was his perpetual friend, Happiness?

Don Lino raised his head:

"I have to confess that I've been naïve. Now I'm starting to be afraid of everything to do with Japan."

Don Ramon pounded his fist on the table. With Japan...?

"It has the habit of puffing up things in its favor with the most picturesque fables and the most smashing lies. And it's trying to frighten everybody while it's scared to death itself. It's like those cowardly little boys who go into a room at night and belt out screams to hide their fear. Take a good look at them: they're all horrible. Shoguns, Daimyos, Samurai. They even try to frighten us with their own gods, presenting them with the monstrous faces of dogs and devils, when those gods of theirs, in human form, at least the ones on the fringes of their immoral mythology, were a bunch of poor bastards..."

Take, for example, the one that's right in front of you, the potbellied, roly-poly one with a clown's face and his belly button sticking up. That half-wit, Daibutsu. What modern-day Asia has made of the poor fellow... Speak, Guatama. Tell them not to be frauds. That you are the most beautiful of princes and the most elegant of mortals. That you fled your palace overflowing with music, flowers, lights and beautiful slave-girls who barely dared press their lips to your sandals of pearls, because above all else, you loved liberty, feeling, without that liberty, more unhappy than the birds and the clouds. That you exchanged your regal garb for a coarse sackcloth, and your fine sword, as luminous as a moonbeam, for a crude pilgrim's staff. That you foreswore the happiness they lied to you about, because you understood that happiness, like love, is a poet's dream. And that you yourself, and by yourself, became a god when you renounced all splendor and glory, and bowed your head while you opened your heart to the only three great truths of life: illness, old age, and death.

Don Lino didn't seem to hear what his brother was going on about. He was still lost in thought, far from all reality, with his head buried in the palms of his hands. Suddenly he seemed to wake up. He took a piece of yellow paper from the table and held it out with a grimace that he tried to make into a smile:

"Take this, Ramon. Look it over..."

And Don Ramon read:

"Kyoto, 14 September 1941
Mr. Lino Robles.
Manila.
My most esteemed and generous protector:
The cherry trees have blossomed five times, and during all that time our fates have been like the wings of an egret, stroking in union, but always apart.

I am extremely thankful for your kind remembrance, but I must implore you not to think of me again, and to forget me forever. I am no longer yours. I do not even belong to myself. I have been Mrs. Nitobe for a year now, and my honorable husband and I are expecting a beautiful baby very soon.

I hope you will be able to excuse your humble servant.
Haruko.

He threw the paper down on the table contemptuously.
Don Lino, pale, dared to ask:
"What do you have to say about that..."
Don Ramon drew himself up, arms crossed, and looked at his brother with a sort of disdain mixed with pathetic, sad pity:
"What do you want me to tell you? The same thing you told me not long ago when you were praising your great love of loves. 'If you ever need a loving lady at your side, look for a Japanese woman...!'"

V

Master Anselmi set about bad-mouthing Natalia in front of his pupils. She had the voice of a frog; she sang like a dog; and if this wasn't enough, she was carrying on with an Asian boy who was more of an ape than Othello.

Maybe it was due to his physical appearance that that womanizer seemed to hate men of classical attractiveness, among whom the musician considered himself an exceptional model. And just so that he wouldn't have to throw him off the balcony one day, he stopped giving lessons to the Robles girl. Why come down from his Olympic peak? A superior man, from a superior race, a musician of world-wide fame, an incomparable artist? Besides which, the blood that ran through his veins wasn't the same as that of other mortals. Everyone else's was red. His was blue.

This ridiculous personal propaganda, in the style of Gayda[60] and Brunetti,[61] amalgamated in a pile of insults, by some miracle didn't reach Natalia's ears. Since Anselmi did not hold back the name of the one he was hurling his invectives against, Natalia's friends shared them with that perverse pleasure that women have of welcoming such tales.

But Kauffman accidentally came to hear about it, and he exchanged some strong words with his "ally."

"I consider myself like a part of that family, and I won't allow you to offend it that way. You keep your tongue stuck to the piano, or you're going to find my fist in your snout. I'm not so old that I can't pound a little music theory into you. We Germans are better musicians than the lot of you."

Anselmi wasn't going to let himself be cowed by somebody that he didn't think had any reason to meddle in his affairs. And Kauffman couldn't do anything but stomach his irate remonstration.

"Save your fists for the English and the Russians, my dear doctor. And just so you'll know, I'm not a man to put up with threats. If you respect the Robles family, so do I. The only things I've said is that the bambina shouldn't waste her time making herself out to be a skylark. And that the Chinaman she has for a shield is an 'animale indefinido.'"

Ma, wait...! Wait...! You're a Nazi and I'm a Fascist, and we shouldn't fight at this sacrosanct time when Italy and Germany are fighting on the same side, looking ahead to glory. The individual should disappear for the sake of the nation. And the 'individuale' pride should be sacrificed for the love of the country.

The masterly thrust was able to penetrate into the patriotic feelings of Hitler's underling. And in Kauffman's myopic eyes there glowed the red, tattered vision of the fields of battle in poor Europe.

He was almost sorry for having provoked the professor over some idle gossip. He was a friend, an ally, a comrade. The Anselmis over there were on the same side as the Kauffmans, bombing cities, leveling lands, sticking their bayonet into the bare chest of divine liberty. You had to exterminate all the enemy races. Not even leave the women behind, because the next day they could give birth to future avengers. Slaughter the children, new enemies as soon as they became men. Death and destruction to all of them, burn them all. Only one master power on the face of the earth, Germany. And at the feet of Germany, to dust off its boots, happy to be alive, grateful, submissive, Italy and Japan.

"All right, maestro, I'm a German above all else. I take back what I just said to you. Let's shake hands..."

And they each went their own way, stomping their feet so hard that an echo came back from the sidewalk.

On that day, Kauffman paid Don Lino a visit. Apparently, Kyoto's letter had upset Robles' stomach. He couldn't handle the bitterness. When the golden Japanese temple came crashing down, it tore at his heart. Ridiculous heart of an old man who seemed to love his "musme" as never before, now that he had lost her forever.

Goodbye, lofty, sacred notion of woman with a face like a full moon! Just like the light of the moon, her light was false. Farewell, intoxicating illusion of a beautiful rebirth inside the silks and incense of a transparent house, resting on his haunches like a Buddha in adoration of a Haruko strumming the "koto"[62] and warbling like a sparrow. The song of the "geishas"[63] who know how to love only once in their lifetime! Goodbye, murmuring canopy of cedars and eucalyptus trees, green candelabra of the sun! Farewell, caresses that smell like flowers of the plum tree! Farewell, love!

Everything was gone, fantasy and hope, dove and nest, idol and faith. Ahead of him lay only the sad panorama of a lonely old age and abandoned affections, shut up in this modern chateau in Manila, or in the ancient ramshackle house on the farm, with no more pleasure or consolation than this garden that was withering away here, and the fields further on, full of birds and twigs...

"What's wrong with me, Fritz?"

"You're sixty years old and you're suffering from a nervous depression that we have to take care of, no matter what. If we neglect this illness, you'd come down with neurasthenia. And from there, it's only one step away from dementia."

Don Lino gave a start:

"Fritz, don't be a barbarian!"

Kauffman spoke calmly:

"Don't deny that you were rowdy when you were young, that you overdid it in life, and even today you have more of a taste for females than you do for cooked rice…"

"Man, that…!"

"That's where this comes from. And you have to take care of it. Tell me, was there something that really upset you recently?"

Don Lino hesitated for a moment. Then he exclaimed resolutely:

"There have been a lot of unsettling things, Fritz. The people on this estate, for one thing, have gotten into discussing politics, and whether or not the war is coming here, and so they're taking advantage of the situation to get up to their old tricks. Natalia is getting married and leaving me behind. Fernando is going too; I don't know whether it's to be married or to let himself be sacrificed like a lamb. And as if that wasn't enough, take a look at this letter I just got from Japan…"

"From the 'geisha'?"

Don Lino nodded.

And Kaufmann said:

"I understand about Natalia and Fernando and what's happening out on the fields. The first may be painful and the second a great disappointment. But you have no reason to be troubled about the last thing. An Asian woman is just like all other women. Eyes that don't see, a heart with no feelings. And in ninety-nine percent of the cases, a heart without feelings even if the eyes see."

"That's too much, Fritz!..."

"Look, Lino, a man who stakes his happiness on a woman's love, has something wrong with his head. A woman is like a chocolate bonbon. Very pretty and appetizing while it's inside the golden tinfoil. But as soon as you take off its shiny wrapper and put it in your mouth, you dirty your fingers and smudge your lips. It tastes very good: no doubt about that. But it always leaves you wanting more when it doesn't turn out to be overly gooey."

Don Lino, visibly at a loss, tried to defend himself:

"It's because our race is so romantic...! It's the oriental blood...! It's that we Filipinos feel things in a different way from the rest of you...!"

"Cock and bull!" thundered Kauffman. "As a matter of fact, you Filipinos are more polygamous than Solomon![64] That business about only one woman forever and ever is a notion of tacky novelists over here. In the matter of women, what's most important is the quantity. Quality is just a fleeting cloud."

"But even in harems there are favorites... It's that your metaphysics..."

"It's the philosophy of love! The minute you can prove to me that there ever existed one single man, from Adam up till you, that hasn't seen all women as their favorites, that's when I'll let them slit open my jugular vein."

"There have been cases..."

"There have been canary birds! From the beginning of the world, some other woman is always preferable to one's own. Because of something in the laws of Moses, our neighbor's wife is forbidden to us.

something in the laws of Moses, our neighbor's wife is forbidden to us. Man is always the hardest animal to please. And if you don't think so, look at this! A man who has a fat wife, likes skinny women; if a man's wife is short, he's crazy for the tall ones, and vice-versa; when he gets tired of a white woman, he falls in love with all the dark-skinned ones, and vice-versa; and when his wife is young, he's dying for the old ones; and when his wife is old, he's itching to get his hands on young ones!"

That blessed Haruko is a tiny, little thing, isn't she? Well, now it's up to you to have a fling with a statuesque one. Skinny, right? You'll see how a thick-set one suits you better. Young, isn't she? There are a lot of adorable old ones. Autumn is the most beautiful season of the year. All the leaves fall from the vines. And everything looks golden.

Don Lino turned in his seat.

"Thus spoke Nietzsche, Also sprach Zarathustra!"[65]

"Thus speaks reason! Thus speaks life!"

So then, and with all this, it was eleven o'clock in the morning, and his throat felt like dry paper, and it was hot as hell. Where was that lady beer?

As soon as they brought it, he downed two glasses, breathing sighs of deep satisfaction...

"You may have noticed, Lino, that from the quiet, reserved man I've always been, over the last few days I've become an incorrigible talker. This is due to the fact that I'm finished with science and I'm starting to spend my time as a historian. You have to gather information for future history..."

He was silenced by Fernando, who came in to greet his father. He was coming from the city, preoccupied and sad. Kauffman went up to him:

"How are you doing, general? Have they started loading the cannons yet? Haven't they given the order to aim and fire, by now?"

"Not yet, doctor. But it looks like they're going to give it to us very soon."

Kauffman said something that didn't reach Fernando's ears, because he had gone over to the balcony, and was opening the windowpanes to look out on the sea. So Kauffman, brandishing his third glass of beer like a scepter, went on talking to Don Lino:

"It looks as though the prevailing notion is unanimous: everyone is ready to turn themselves into sacrificial lambs. Despite the fact that you're all aware of what's coming at you, you're just going to face the consequences with the most hare-brained stoicism. A shiny, new acquisition for the religious calendar of Anglo-American war: Saint Philippines, virgin and martyr; innocent and bombed out..."

There followed a silence that Don Lino's voice broke, speaking very softly, as though to himself:

"I remember one day when there was a cockfight, over in town. Two magnificent roosters were going to fight. One of them was white, and the other one yellow. The crowd favorite was the white one. He looked more nervous, stronger, much more of a rooster.

But it happened that when the fight started, the yellow one showed himself to be unexpectedly aggressive, and at the first clash, he was able to slash his rival. That was enough to make the ones who had been hailing the white one as an idol only a minute before, break out, roaring wild curses, taking back bets, pouring insults out on the wounded one. Even though the fight still wasn't over. Dragging itself around bloody in the ring, the white one faced his enemy again. Then the unexpected happened, and it was this: when the yellow one saw that he was being attacked once more, instead of continuing to fight, he ran away like a coward. Meanwhile, in the middle of the ring, in front of the speechless, stunned riffraff, the conqueror, resting on its wings, lifted its crest in a halo of glory.

In the case of America and Japan, I'm afraid that most of the people in the Philippines may do the same thing that took place during the cockfight in my town. When they think the white side is coming out second best, they're going to switch over to the yellow side. I know the psychology of mobs like them, always ready to get down on their knees to the sun that's warmest. And they can call me a bad Filipino for thinking and saying what I think and say. But I won't be the first madman to stick up for the truth.

Fernando was still at the balcony, facing the sea, completely cut off from the conversation swelling behind his back like a murmur. The sun splashed its gold on a cluster of floating cirrus clouds, like foam in space. A white cloud passed by, then another white cloud. A snow-white seagull flew past, then a black kite. And the water, little by little, became filled with sails. Meanwhile, the air was filling with wings.

Front page of the Tribune newspaper of Manila, Philippines with headline of the fall of Bataan, 24 Apr 1942
Source: United States Air Force
Retrieved from: https://ww2db.com/image.php?image_id=4260

PART III

I

The garden was aglow in the night, an immense flame that engulfed all its flowers, all its leaves, launching sparks and reflections of colors into space. Long garlands of paper lanterns and electric bulbs swayed in the wind, chasing away the shadows with their polychromatic waves of light. And the trees, riddled with gleams of light, stood out like burning torches illuminating the flower-lined pathways.

In the background, the palatial mansion seemed to burn as well, in the immense radiance of its lamps. Several orchestras filled the air with music. The guests, in tight-knit groups, began to stream into the house, the gardens…

"The bride and groom…! The bride and groom…!" From a carriage, lost among lilies and orange blossoms, stepped out the bridal couple. Natalia was wrapped in her snow-white regalia, Sandoval donned in a splendid dress-coat. Both appeared happy and radiant, greeting and smiling at everyone. Sandoval, especially, seemed to be bursting with satisfaction.

They had just finished the wedding ceremony, with all the officials and aristocrats from Manila in attendance. Eminent personages and grand ladies sponsored the nuptials. Two clerks had worked several days to finish the guest list. Don Lino wanted to spare no expense. What were the millions for? What was he saving his wealth for? His daughter was getting married!

Marta, dressed in pink and sitting next to Fernando under an acacia that was sparkling like a Christmas tree, felt the celebration throbbing deep in her heart. All the colors of the Japanese lanterns showered down on her, giving her a green head, yellow eyes, red neck, like a wounded dove... Soon there would be another celebration like this, she was thinking. Except that she would be the bride, instead of Natalia. And the groom would be this prince of the enchanted kingdom of her love, who at the present moment was leaning toward her, calling her beautiful and adored...

In a great clearing in the gardens was an extensive space for dancing. Many couples began to dance. Livery-servants walked about everywhere, serving wine and refreshments. Words and laughter arose like a triumphal arch. The pomp was unprecedented. The women flaunted clothing and jewelry whose magnificence was dazzling. Very few weddings would be registered in aristocratic annals to match the great splendor that celebrated the wedding of the daughter of Robles.

While a group of girls from the most elite of society were devouring sandwiches, pastry and wine, they were talking trash about Natalia. As tacky as could be, the conceited thing, with a wedding gown ordered straight out of Hollywood. And what a proud peacock holding up the train! And why on earth all the cockiness? That guy Sandoval could be Confucius in any Chinaman's stall!

Except the tittle-tattle suddenly quieted down because Natalia was walking toward them, greeting them ever so affectionately. And now, stuffed full of liquor and pastry, they began to eat her up with kisses and praises.

She was so gorgeous in her wedding gown, so lively and elegant! And what a wedding hers was, the best of all weddings! And what a nice bridegroom, and how everyone envied him. And what a celebration, this celebration, right out of the Arabian nights...!

Meanwhile, the men were drinking robustly and talking even more robustly about politics and war. They were all turning into strategists and statisticians. When they had drunk enough champagne and were tired of telling whoppers, they went out to dance.

Don Lino was outdoing himself, attending to everyone, doing the honors of the celebration, while Don Ramon was carrying on with several ladies who were feeling romantic as they recalled their blessed wedding days:

"Oh, Don Ramon, say what they may, there is nothing like our times! What times those were! They will never come back now!"

And the things they told...

Back then they had celebrations that lasted days and even weeks, like the wedding of Camacho[66]. When the men got married, they had been in a relationship for at least ten years. They exchanged their first kiss after the Epistle of Saint Paul had tied them together with bonds that only death could undo. And at the crowning moment, the bride had the appearance of a mystical rose, and the groom looked up with helpless eyes.

Everyone at the ceremony cried, as if instead of a wedding they were attending a novena of the blessed souls of purgatory! Some wives even found it prudent and seemly to faint...

"Oh, Don Ramon! What times those were! We'll never see their like again...!

The journalist Andrade, at the head of a group of society reporters, traipsed about everywhere like a grasshopper. He felt completely at home in his professional role, and while gathering information and jotting down notes, he was filling his pockets with cigars and fighting off his inextinguishable thirst with all kinds of wines and liquors. The ladies offered him their best smiles, picturing themselves appearing beautiful and elegant in the columns of "La Linterna." The gentlemen embraced him with friendly pats on the back, treating him as an equal. They knew that Andrade felt grateful to them at times, and that he wouldn't forget them when he wrote his grandiose review of the celebration.

The poor devil! At the expense of his newspaper he was thriving like a magnate and bubbling over like froth on champagne. Something of a psychologist and extremely cynical, he took advantage of human vanity as much as he could. He knew the flaws of every high muck-a-muck and the weakness of every stiff-necked lady. And he was a success as he obsequiously sucked up to everyone, notwithstanding the fact that behind their backs he would immediately drag them through the mud.

"Hey, Andrade...!

"Say, Andrade...!

"Come over here, Andrade...!

They fought over him. And he let himself be touted while thinking of how he would have to stretch his imagination later on with a flood of hyperboles and stunning adjectives to repay all their geniality. Even an old, ugly and sentimental lady who caressed him with her shrill fife of a voice:

"Oh, when you're the one who gets married, Andrade, we'll have another celebration just like this one..."

The poor dummy...! If that miserable thing would poke her nose around the hovel Andrade vegetated in, and mull over the picture of a woman half consumptive from so much hard work, and seven kids who would gobble up the two hundred pesos that he sweated blood for every month, heaping praises on a pack of imbeciles and clodhoppers, there's no doubt she would lay off all that nonsense.

As the night passed by, the orchestras played more clearly vibrantly above the murmurs. The couples were multiplying in a dizzying and suggestive succession of tangos, rhumbas, and exotic dances. Clinging like ivy to a wall, men and women blended sweat and breath, staggering like drunks, leaping around, crawling weakly along the ground. It was a grotesque spectacle, without elegance, rhythm or art. What happened to our dances, the ones grandma danced, swaying like a barely sustained flower, barely revealing beneath the hem of her skirt the small tip of her golden sandal?

The elegant waltz, the sweet mazurka, the languorous polka, all that music as rhythmic as a poem that, more than carnal pleasure, was the lifting of spirit to art, where was it?

In the warm October night, the garden smelled like cinnamon trees and violets. From a climbing plant, some small, white flowers jostled by the breeze fell upon Marta's bosom. She began picking them up with her small fingers to give them to Fernando. He held onto the tiny flowers. And he told her, confident and more in love than ever:

"Even the flowers love you and go looking for you!"

Doctor Kauffman, seated with several of his compatriots at a table filled with glasses and bottles of beer, was speaking in German, while looking with concealed disdain at all the other foreign guests. Barley and hops seemed to have gone to his head a short while ago. Red in the face, almost congested and bathed in sweat, he was fanning himself with a brass platter. The spirits from the beer were firing up his own spirit with unusual patriotism. And before the rows of empty bottles that appeared to him like Nazi mortars dropped from the hands of Hitler to bury the world, feeling like an old-time Bismarck,[67] he stammered bombastically:

"Look at those Japanese guests, neglected and all alone in that group standing over there. All the respect, all the compliments are for the high officials of the Philippines and the American authorities. Idiots! In two or three months' time, they're going to have to crawl down on their knees in front of those yellow dogs, begging for their acknowledgement and a smile."

Kauffman's fellow countrymen mechanically nodded their heads in agreement. And the Doctor continued, saying:

"Japan is entertaining them in Washington with diplomatic proposals, while at the same time they're getting ready to give them a crushing blow. And the people over there, and these people here, are imagining they're in the best of all possible worlds..."

One of the Nazis, bald and with a monocle the size of a dollar in his eye, let out a hearty laugh. The others felt like they ought to do the same. Kauffman, not losing his alcoholic cynicism, continued to pontificate:

"I've been telling that to a lot of Filipinos, but none of them pay a damned bit of attention to me. They have such great hope in their future and undying faith in America that it borders on innocence, if not ignorance. They're deluded, fanatics, convinced they'll be triumphant in war the same way they are in peace. Dreamers! They don't know that when Germany draws its sword, after it sheaths it again there won't be a puppet left with its head still in place. And like us, and with us, Italy and Japan, despite the fact that the Italians are nothing but poultry in a farmyard and the Japanese are a bunch of pigs."

The whistle of a fireworks rocket interrupted Kauffman as it lifted off, zigzagging and exploding in a shower of glitter high in the air. Then other rockets, filled with booms and flashes, ribbons of fire hurled at the clouds to catch the stars. The dancing had stopped and the guests were looking at the flares being launched into the breeze from a remote, hidden place. And in the night, wounded by such radiance, the rockets were butterflies that died out, burning their wings in the high flame of the stars.

With his lips, Fernando directed Marta's attention to a castle that had just been lit. There appeared two hearts, united and transfixed by an arrow. They were glowing in the center of a ring of flowers that were spinning and leaving petals in dripping glitter and golden flashes of lightning...

"Look at how love is burning, look...! Those are supposed to be the hearts of Natalia and Sandoval...! And the dazzling halo encircling them, all the promises they have made to each other, and all the hopes they have dreamed...! Fireworks, colored lights, love!"

She looked at him in astonishment:

"Why are you saying those things?"

He quelled her unease in an instant.

"Not our love! Your heart and my heart can't burn that way, like sparklers that, after they flare up, die out. Ours burn like stars that, instead of being consumed by their fire, glow forever."

Don Lino had drawn apart from all the hubbub and was wandering along a tree-lined pathway. Without knowing why, he was sad, his heart was troubled and he felt like crying.

Suddenly he felt Natalia clinging to him.

"We're leaving, Papa..."

It was growing late and, taking advantage of the moments when the guests were distracted, watching the fireworks, they were slipping away. They needed to spend the entire night on the road in their car if they hoped to get to Baguio[68] before dawn. The exact time when they could change clothes at home, and then, on their way.

"Goodbye, Papa..."

Sandoval took the hand that Don Lino stretched out to him.

"Goodbye, Papa."

"God bless you both... Goodbye..."

He watched them leave hurriedly, and disappear among the lights and shadows, happy, gleeful, like children ditching school, like birds freed from their cage, without looking back, intoxicated with the egoism of their passion and their freedom.

And he let himself slump down on a hidden, solitary bench while the last flashes of fireworks were dying out and the melodious rhythms of the orchestra faintly reached out to him.

Natalia had finally gone. He no longer had a daughter. And these were the laws of life, sir. Care for her like a rosebud, tenderly and jealously, until she becomes an enchanting flower. So that then the first strapping young lad who passes by cuts her from the vine, and takes her away? To where? Happiness? It's almost always to pain, since love and life are pain...

My dear child! He could picture her now the day she was born, when she uttered her first words, when she took her first steps. He could see her now, growing up, becoming a little girl, becoming a woman, the way a rosebush grows, climbing until it reaches the heights with its roses. She was always the little one, pampered by her mother, spoiled by her father, the baby doll, the joy of the house. What wouldn't he have done for that daughter, bending always to all her fancies and whims, having never denied her anything, not even this wedding that still didn't convince him, that still did not fill his soul.

She had gone, after all, without realizing how heart-broken he was at her leaving him, without justifying her ingratitude, for leaving aside being always what she once was, a ray of sunshine, a baby doll, a lilting skylark...

He felt a sudden shiver running through his entire body. He dabbed at his eyes with a handkerchief...

And he noticed, in resignation, that he was becoming overwhelmed with sobbing.

III

Delicate, ample bosom; colossal and gigantic bosom veiled by the floating gossamer of its vegetation; bosom of woman, of Mother Earth to which the clouds descend to drink in the colors, the volcano Arayat rises under the firmament, silhouetted lofty and alone in space.

At its feet there stretch thousands of acres that make up the Robles estate. Enormous rice paddies with upright sprigs like golden swords; infinite numbers of sugarcane plants spiked with green stars. In the far distance, steam-driven mills, locker rooms, the workers' houses. And even farther away, standing out lost in the trees like a tall, white, shining temple, the mansion of Don Lino, surrounded by parks and gardens.

The house, which had closed up a month before due to the absence of its inhabitants, has come to life again. Inside are Don Lino and Don Ramon, who had come a few days after Natalia's wedding. The movement of servants and workers is unusual. The owners have arrived, and the farmhand disturbances are over.

Don Lino, armed with a large gun meant to intimidate, goes out on horseback, riding over his lands. Don Ramon takes charge of the offices. Law and order come back to prevail everywhere.

The old man needed this. The outdoors, the scent of mountain air, physical and mental exercise. He seemed to have grown years older in the last two months. He was no longer the romantic dreamer of languorous, sinful "musmes," no longer was he the zealous champion of a turbulent Asia; now he was becoming filled with new dreams and and responsibilities in life, and he was beginning not to give a damn about the past or the future.

He owed his existence to the present, and he was devoting his life to the present. Let the brutes knock each other's block off, and let the women offer themselves to whomever they wanted. Just let him have his horse, the sun, the fields and the deep, peaceful sleep of a child every night.

Today he was feeling more optimistic and elated than ever. He had just read, reread, and read again a letter from Sandoval that gave him two pieces of unexpected news. That Natalia was pregnant, and that they were coming down from Baguio to be with him all the time that he and uncle Ramon would be staying at his estate.

He went through all the rooms, looking for his brother:

"Ramon...! Hey, Ramon...!"

Until finally he found him in his office, sorting through seventy different samples of rice:

"Great news...! Wonderful news...! Look at what Sandoval wrote!"

Don Ramon left the samples aside to read the letter.

"What a Natalia, old boy...! Congratulations!"

What a Natalia...!

What a Philippine woman! What a treasure of pure, bountiful flesh, ardent and fertile like the earth from which she is formed, where tendrils sprout even among the stones, and flowers grow even on shafts of thorns!

"Can you imagine anything greater than this? Natalia, expecting! A baby on the way!"

As he laughed, his eyes filled with tears. Don Ramon, in turn overcome with emotion, hypothesized very seriously:

"In nine months, one! And in nine years, ten! All this, without counting the future factory of Fernando! And you were wandering around feeling sad and lonely because you thought you were all alone, abandoned in the world. Two left, and they'll bring you twenty!"

A baby, a little boy, his daughter's son! The daughter of his life, a thousand times blessed! Don Lino did not know what to do, or to say. For now he was going to send a radiogram to Baguio, telling them to come immediately. There was nowhere else that she would be safer or better cared for than here. They needed to look out for their treasure.

Little one...! Little one...! He would be named Lino, like himself, and he would take care of him, of course! That's why he was his grandfather! And that's why it would be him, and no one else, that was going to take care of him and make him into a man, right? Every inch a man, Ramon!

"And instead of a boy, what if it turns out to be a girl?"

"Don't get my goat! If it's a girl, we'll call her Ramona! And you'll take care of her!"

Shortly afterward, Father Elías came in, all sweaty and out of breath, humbly holding out a list of things they needed for the church. A new chasuble, because the old one was falling to pieces; strings for the harmonium which was completely mute; two broken pulpit angels; an alms box for the souls in purgatory; the prayer book that termites had eaten; and four silver candlesticks that had been stolen...

"What wicked people, Mr. Don Lino! Imagine: even taking things off the altar! And I never stop preaching to them every day about precepts, about the holy commandments, especially the seventh, to make them understand how ugly that crime is. And nothing! No matter if you preach to them in Spanish, in Pampango,[69] in English or even in Latin! They don't understand anything about sermons! One of these days they're going to make off with the saints the same way they take sacks of rice whenever they can! What wicked people, Mr. Don Lino!"

Don Lino smiled:

"Don't worry, Father; it will all be taken care of. In fact, I was just thinking of giving you two thousand pesos to have them fix up the chapel and give it a fresh coat of paint. I didn't like the way it was looking last Sunday. Ask the manager for the money, and have them start working on it as soon as possible."

Father Elías fastened his eyes full of gratitude on the old man's eyes.

"Thank you, Don Lino. May the Lord keep this in mind, since it is all for the greater glory of God. But allow me to say that I think the amount is really too much..."

"No, sir. You fix the church up for me so it's as bright as a pin. And if you need any more money, tell me. I want it all to look new and shining. We are going to have a great baptism..."

The priest bowed:

"That being so, praise God. And I want to say again, thank you."

The good parish priest was about to leave, when Don Lino stopped him:

"Ah, I forgot to ask you something very important. How are you fixed for the bells?"

"We have two: one is very big and the other one is smaller…"

"Do they ring all right? They're not cracked?"

"No, sir; they ring very nicely."

"All right, it doesn't matter. Let's see if we can arrange it so that instead of having two, you'll have four. And they'll chime out like the devil! So they can be heard more than five miles away!"

Ah, little one…! When they anoint your little mug with salt, then you'll see how the bells are going to peal out so much that they'll bring the whole belfry down! On my word as a Robles, little one!

He stood there, watching him come down through the air, still so high, so high that he couldn't make him out. Two storks were bringing him, fast asleep, between their white wings. It would still take nine months before he got there, the sky was so far up. Since he was so small, they would have to bring him slowly, very carefully, little by little, just so they wouldn't trip over a star, a cloud, an aurora. He had to arrive hale and hearty, strong and strapping. That was what the good Lord commanded, and what the good Lord ordered had to be done.

Don Ramon broke through his reverie:

"What are you thinking about, with your head in the clouds?"

"That I have an enormous appetite. You and I are going to treat ourselves to a big, fat pork belly, right now!"

They went into the dining room together:

"What an enormous change has come over you all of a sudden, Lino. You look like a new man."

"I need to live!"

"Life is here, right here, on your own land, with your loved ones, not way over there where you imagined it, in that setting of fans and the paper pagoda of that Japanese dove of yours. You needed to have a bitter lesson about infidelity and ingratitude from an Asian actress to wake you up to the reality of your life. And now, to return yourself to the honor and well-being of living, the present that your daughter is giving you is about to arrive. Because, and don't deny it: you're not so old as not to go all soppy that way. Before he left, Father Elías asked me what great baptism we were going to have. You gave orders for the church to be set up as though for an extraordinary event..."

"He told you that, huh? And what else did he say?..."

"Well, that now, more than ever, he needs a new chasuble."

Don Lino burst out laughing. He would have his chasuble, and he would even have a cathedral as soon as the child descended from the clouds. He was going to be an extraordinary little boy, Ramon!

Two days later the newlyweds arrived. They were coming in an automobile loaded down with suitcases and containers, and they had in tow another car filled with fruit, flowers and plants from Baguio. Before she stepped out onto the ground, Natalia was crying out happily:

"Papa, I'm bringing you pine trees and cypresses...! And strawberries and gladiolas and carnations and roses...! We've been perfuming all the roads along the way!... Papa, how glad I am to see you...!"

She jumped down like a bird and clung to her father, smothering him with kisses. She looked more nimble and thinner than ever, and her color was much better. Don Lino looked at her in astonishment. How could that be? And the baby? Where was the baby? He could see no sign in the woman of the sweet miracle of the incarnation. Had she brazenly lied just so that his famous son-in-law could put on airs?

He took him aside while Natalia was talking to her uncle.

"What you wrote about your wife's condition, is that true? Are you sure? You're not mistaken?"

Sandoval laughed:

"For God's sake, how could I be mistaken? Or did you forget that I'm a medical doctor?"

"But you can hardly notice..."

"Of course not, three weeks! But you'll be seeing it pretty soon... As soon as you see her swallow down strawberries, by the handfuls, with salt!"

Don Lino shivered with delight:

"So then, strawberries, huh...?"

After they had exchanged a few words, Sandoval seemed to become shrouded in a cloud of melancholy. Bad news from Manila. Constant testing of defenses every night; the Philippine army integrated with the American army and all the troops mobilized; preparations for war at every turn; the conflict, seemingly inevitable, awaited with anxiety from one day to the next...

"I'm afraid they're going to call me up. Almost all my colleagues are in the lines... Don't you get the newspapers from Manila? Haven't you read the latest cablegrams?"

They got the newspaper, but they never read it. Besides, if anything happened that was important or serious, Fernando would let them know. Although Don Lino was still optimistic...

"I can't imagine it happening, no matter how hard I try; it's impossible for me to believe such a thing; something in my heart tells me that it's not going to happen, that it couldn't happen."

Don Ramon smiled ironically:

"Still got an itch for that filly from Nikko, huh?

The old man protested, looking nervously toward Natalia:

"No, man! It's a gut-feeling!"

"Well, tell that gut that it's lying, Lino."

Sandoval weighed in:

"I think those people will behave respectably. I've lived with them in Tokyo for three years, and nothing has led me to believe that they would be anything other than honorable. They are guided, every last one of them, by the Bushido,[70] the religion of all the people, the devotion to honor."

Don Ramon sat up in his seat:

"Oh, the Bushido, the great, incomparable, stupendous Bushido...! I know it by heart...! Do you want to hear me spout its maxims...? Listen..."

When destiny places you face to face with your lord and master, his Imperial Majesty, the son of his mother and a descendant in direct lineage of all the gods there ever were or ever will be out in the Boonies, bow your head down to the belly button, and don't dare look up at the divine being, because if you don't die from fear after seeing his divine image, hundreds of sabers will fall on your neck, and your head will pass into history.

If a geisha cobbles together a son for you, set him aside for cannon wadding. If it's a girl, as soon as she's off the pacifier, sell her to the red-light district of Yoshiwara. And with the money they give you for her, apply yourself to business, farming or fishing.

If, instead of being the daughter of a geisha, she turns out to be the daughter of a princess, don't sell her because people would take a dim view of a transaction like that. Marry her off to an honorable member of the General Staff of the Imperial Forces; that way the mother, the father and all the other relatives of your illustrious son-in-law will have a maid that they can unload their rage and work onto.

When some poor bugger steals a goose from you, tie him up tight to a post, and beat him and kick him until he comes apart at the seams. You need to make him understand that according to the law of force, the only force of our law, that just as a man who steals a pearl necklace deserves to be hailed as a hero, someone who steals a chicken needs to be crushed to death like a Chinaman.

Get drunk constantly and continually. Have all your pores smell of saké. And when you find yourself with your true personality, spurting out your divine spirit through your mouth, your ears and your nose, remember that you are a privileged, unique and incomparable being, and squat down to give thanks to the glorious shades of your forebears.

You have no father, no mother, no dog that howls. You have only the Emperor. If, for any reason, you can't love him, serve him, worship him and sanctify him for all that he merits and deserves, grab a corkscrew and pull out your guts. What do you want guts for? They're the most despicable part of man!

If you can't be a Grand Marshal or an Admiral to exterminate the Chinese rats, yoke yourself onto the shafts of a kuruma, which amounts to the same thing. And make yourself into a human rack, because it was you who were born for that, and not the horse, the mule, the burro, the ass...

He was suddenly silent, blinded by the red flash of a streak of lightning, and stunned by the great rumbling crash of thunder. For some time an enormous cloud had been darkening the sky, blocking out the sun. Natalia jumped up in fright.

"How terrible, it struck right out there, in the garden... It knocked down that acacia..."

Another blinding light, another terrible boom, and after a blast of wind that rattled the doors and windows, a heavy torrent of rain began to pound down.

Don Lino stood up nervously:

"You see, Ramon? You've offended the divine Empire. The Asian Gods are answering your mockery. We're going to have thunder and lightning for a while now..."

III

Fernando wrote from Manila, confirming the alarming news that Sandoval had anticipated. In the city a disquieting sense of unease began to arise, due to the preparations for defense ordered by the authorities and the turn of events that seemed to be taking place in the diplomatic activity of the Foreign Affairs Department. Prince Konoe[71] had fallen from power, along with the entire ministry, and in his place Tokyo was announcing a new cabinet, headed by Tojo.[72]

The military party was in power. It was war. The pair of traveling gramophones, with the brand name of Nomura and Kurusu,[73] who were wandering around Washington, puzzling over the recordings of peace and good will, turned out to be a couple of fake, lying, cynical noisemakers. Japan was more prepared for war than anyone could imagine. And the first blow could be struck when no one at all was suspecting it.

So there were no delusions. The story of the wolf was nearing its end. The beast would suddenly appear. You could hear him howling, you noticed his contemptible scurrying, you sensed his sly, bloodthirsty drive. On the hands of time, in the course of destiny, in the heart of the Philippines the terrible hour was going to strike.

War...!

Cities razed, fields laid waste, women raped, children and old people reduced to ash. Blood and desolation everywhere. Grief and pain on every road. The good God was going to close His eyes, and while the good God had his eyelids shut, the apocalyptic beast from the vision of John would burst out, breaking its seals one by one, to flood the land of the Philippines with horror and fear.

Fernando's letter, addressed to his father, was read aloud to the family without comment of any sort. They all held a deep silence. On all the faces one could feel sad thoughts. What would become of all the people, all the homes, the soldiers themselves, the ones from America and our own, who were in training for battle, marching together to the places of danger, under the waving flags soaring on high.

According to technicians and experts and critics and prominent military strategists, the Philippines was an indefensible country. They would need the combined squadrons of the most powerful countries, air forces with thousands upon thousands of planes, and millions of armed men to guard and protect their seas, their skies, their thousands of islands. Did they have any of that in the country? The only thing they had was great courage, high moral standards, and a unanimous and unsparing desire to show to America, to the world, that the Filipinos would carry out their duty.

With the apparent nearness of danger, Don Lino relapsed into memories of Japan. He wasn't bothered by the deceit of the beloved "musme" of another time. The wound of this romantic treachery had healed over completely. He admired Japan, and he could not help it. He still had the conviction that its people were worthy of the highest regard and esteem. His blood had been poisoned by the liquor of its Asiatic voluptuousness, and his spirit was unsettled by the fascination of its legends and its landscapes. What mattered least was the treachery of a forsaken geisha. In her case, any other woman of any other race could have done the same. The real guilty party was himself, since he had abandoned her.

Except that he could not express his feelings or his thoughts out loud. Everything around him was hostile to anything that smelled Japanese. You only had to mention the name "Japan" to unleash a mountain of expletives. It was the masked friend of yesterday, the avowed aggressor of the present, the unknown despot of the future. No, he couldn't defend it now; he was alone against everyone, millions of eyes saw only a horrible beast in what seemed to him a siren of overabundant enchantment.

They had no love for Japan, they couldn't love it because they didn't know it the way he did. And they were not afraid of it because they didn't know its strength and its power. But for Don Lino and several other Filipinos who had lived there and had the chance to peer into its interior and discover the exuberant, breathtaking life that throbbed there, Japan was an enemy to be feared as much as, or more than, Germany itself. In every bourgeois, in every prince, in every villager, in every spokesman of science and art, there breathed a soldier. And what soldiers! A troop of suicidal fanatics who went into battle with their necks bowed, their eyes closed, and advancing, advancing, always advancing, thinking more enthusiastically of death than of life.

He could see them now, triumphant, marching down the magnificent avenues of the capital like swarms of frogs, small, shorn, squat, bow-legged. And after them, the invasion. Thousands of women like painted butterflies, anxious to settle on any branch; millions of men, rotting away from hunger in its parishes and in its villages, and arriving on our shores, tremulous with dreams of wealth, with illusions of personal well-being. Poor people, but simple and good, thought Don Lino. They were really pitiful! You even felt like you wanted to help them and go to their aid...! Sad people, misunderstood and great. No, he would never have the heart, no matter what happened, to hate them. He saw no more to blame in the Asiatic Empire than that of sinking its teeth and its nails into the white, steely hands of those who were unjustly trying to strangle it.

Ramon's voice came to break through his strange thoughts:
"What shall we do, Lino?"
"You tell me."
"We have ninety-thousand pesos on hand that we haven't been able to deposit in the Bank; the storehouses are full of rice and sugar; the workers are leaving their houses and abandoning us, walking off the fields and into God knows what hells, some of them afraid of war, and most of them because they're socialists; work will shut down for days, for hours, I don't see any way for us to go on like this..."

Don Lino brushed his hand across his forehead:
"Shut down all the work. What else can we do! Whatever hasn't been harvested, let it stay the way it is. We have to resign ourselves to getting ready for whatever may come. If war comes here, it won't last long. Everything will be straightened out afterward."

"And in the meantime, we..."
Don Lino took a deep breath:
"We, at least I, are not moving out of here. And Natalia's staying with me. And her husband, unless they force him into service! I suppose that you'll be staying too."
"And you suppose right. I'll stay. Where else can I go?"
But that night an urgent telegram came from Fernando, and Don Ramon had to return to Manila. Someone needed to go there to take care of the house. Captain Robles received orders to report to the army within twenty-four hours.

This unexpected blow seemed to unnerve Don Lino. He began to lose heart, and fell into a deep despondency. That son had set out to upset him terribly, and at last he had gotten his way. Now, more than ever, he ought to be near, to be with his family, without that damned obligation to get himself involved in the barbaric slaughter that was drawing near...

His only consolation was Natalia, taking refuge now in the paternal hearth, with that child sleeping inside her. He couldn't be near her without glancing unobtrusively at her belly. When would her breasts begin to fill out? When would lines begin to come apart and slimness pass from the virginal flesh? When would the glorious seal of sublime maternity reveal itself? When would you begin to show signs of life, little one?

Just as he was awaiting his grandson with wild anxiety now, that was how he had looked forward to his own son when his saintly wife revealed the news to him, crying shyly and happily as she found shelter in his arms and in his heart. The great Fernando! Before he was born, he already loved him more than his own life! And this was his reward; this was the gratitude and payment he got for his love; leaving him alone, abandoned, at a time of danger, to go and fight for a romantic dream of liberty and glory.

Don Lino, like many other well-heeled Filipinos, did not sympathize with the Americans, nor did he agree with their policy of making the country independent. He was repelled by anything that smelled of internal or external politics. And he only took notice of the grave matter of an ill-timed, dangerous game they were playing in which they would all come out badly. Independence meant the ruin of the Philippine people. The only ones who could want it were the four exalted puppets who would benefit from it. But not the people. The people were not, and would not be prepared for a long time for such a great responsibility. The masses could only call for their rights, every step of the way, completely ignoring their responsibilities. They took advantage of the freedoms they were granted with indecent impunity. And they wandered around their lands, torn apart, divided into political parties and religious factions, turning on each other at every moment, quarreling and wielding as a crushing argument the fratricidal dagger. Thinking that they were doing us a great favor, America was doing us a grave injury. And if God did not straighten it out in time, it was getting ready to cause us an even greater harm. Giving us complete and absolute freedom in '46. Putting in the hands of a mischievous child a bomb of dynamite.

If Japan came, that would be the salvation of the Philippines. The bitter lessons they might give us, would be the finish of the licentiousness of our customs, of the lack of responsibility in our life. The country needed a stern master, a dictatorial policy, a firm hand to guide it to the highest of destinies and the worthiest endeavors. Until now the government of the Philippines had been a government of light opera. And the nation that imagined itself created in the image and likeness of the one across the seas, was a willing victim of the greatest sort of self-deception... So, Japan was coming. For Don Lino, all the better; it was very welcome. Let it come, the sooner, the better.

But the one who came was Kauffman. He was on his way to Baguio, and he wanted to spend the night at the country house. He wanted to talk, he needed to talk to his old friend:

"I suppose you've heard about the terrible situation."

Don Lino shrugged:

"Fernando wrote something..."

Kauffman bellowed out:

"Fernando doesn't know a damn thing; not one of you knows anything; the Japanese are in the Philippines with their fleet, with their airplanes, with their transports full of mortars, tanks, men..."

Don Lino blanched:

"How can that be...? Who has seen them...?"

Kauffman made a scornful face:

"No one has seen them because you're all blind. But I can swear to it, and when I give you my word it's because I have it on the highest authority."

Robles shrugged again:

"All right, very well. It had to come sometime."

The German doctor appeared to be bursting with pride and arrogance. Thundering out his hard, weighty words as though they were cannonballs, he continued:

"I warned you from the very beginning that this war wouldn't be anything like the last one; that the time had come to remake the world map; that before Germany, nothing, and after Germany, no one. Victory will be ours, Lino, and after our victory..."

He hesitated for a few seconds, and then continued resolutely:

"After our victory, we'll make Italy polish our boots, and when they're nice and shiny, we'll give Japan a couple of kicks in the rear. Us first, us second, and us third."

Germany has a lot of old scores to settle, a lot of claims to make, and now the time has come to collect. These yellow Nips can be a great help to us right now, in spite of the fact that we'll have to make them toe the line later on. They're very strong and resolute. Straight off, they can give the English a good clobbering; time will tell, you'll see.

Don Lino was silent, deep in thought. Kauffman went on arrogantly:

"The only thing England has is their pride, and the Americans have nothing but the dollar. The wars of today aren't won with gold or vanity, even if there are dumbbells around who think like Napoleon that all you need to win a war is money. No, sir. Wars today are scientific, and men are the least of it. There you have Japan, poorer than a rat. Poorer than a rat, and you'll see how it wallops."

A servant interrupted them, announcing to Don Lino that some military men were paying a call. The old man, startled by such an untimely visit at this hour, had them come inside:

"How may I help you?"

An American lieutenant explained.

They were very sorry to be a bother, but they were just given orders to arrest a citizen of an enemy country who was at this moment in his house.

Don Lino looked at Kauffman:

"I don't understand... Are you saying, you mean the doctor?... My friend, Doctor Kauffman, who is standing right here?"

"Yes, sir."

"But has war been declared already? Is it because...?" Robles tried to protest weakly.

The officer stood at attention.

"I'm sorry, but I can't give you any explanation... Good evening."

And Don Lino, powerless, astonished and heavy-hearted, saw how Kauffman, the great Kauffman, was taken away from his home under arrest. And all the time that this was taking place, the doctor, pale and trembling, had not opened his mouth even to breathe.

Oh, these Germans. Oh, that caste of demigods who were going to remake the map of the world and change the face of the universe.

IV

They left them alone on the veranda, facing the garden, with the last lights of dusk falling away sadly. A sweet scent of magnolias reached out to them, pervading their sorrow. He had come to say goodbye. Urgent orders to report to the regiment. And fallen to his knees before her, holding her tightly in his arms, he looked at her fervently, he looked at her a long while, as if he were trying to pull out her soul with his eyes, and carry in his eyes her beloved image forever.

"You need to be brave, my dear Marta!"

"Yes."

"Don't you cry! Don't let grief drag you down!"

"No!"

"You'll wait for me patiently, confidently. And when I come back victorious, we'll fulfill our dream, this hope of our life that war is taking from us today."

On her bosom there shone a medallion of the Sacred Heart, as it hung from a tiny chain that she had just fastened around her neck. Now she handed him her golden rosary:

"Don't let go of it. Keep it with you always! Pray to it every day! You'll see how the Holy Virgin saves you!"

She was pale, deathly pale. One could say that the blood of her very being had flowed into her heart, and that her flesh was that of the magnolias that were quivering in the night, or of the stars that were beginning to shine brightly.

Cold and white, like those sleeping queens of stone sculpted on the imperial tombs. Cold and white, like the froth of a wave that is about to break, like a snowy handkerchief that is waving goodbye...

"You'll come back soon. Heaven tells me so."

Her voice sounded teary, as it tore apart from her lips. He assured her, yes, that heaven was telling her the truth. He would be back soon; he couldn't die.

"It's just that if they kill you, they'll be killing me, Nando!"

They were silent for a long while, not finding words of hope and strength to say to each other. She, in particular, was beginning to falter. She saw her beloved far away, lost in the fray, and all their dreams fallen apart. The little house that awaited them like a nest, when would it be filled with its lullaby? And her regalia of a bride, all that white gossamer smelling of roses and the flesh of angels, when would she wear them to give herself to love like a queen, like a woman, like a slave?

As though he could divine her sad thoughts, he tried to follow her lead, reassuring her:

"I can't die! Do you know why? Because I'm not afraid!"

She moaned:

"Oh, it's for that very reason, because I know you're not afraid! The first ones to fall are always the ones who aren't afraid of anything..."

He cut her off, protesting loudly:

"No! That's an absurd idea. To prove you wrong, I'm going to tell you about something that happened to me one time, and that you haven't heard about..."

It happened once, a long time ago, when he and another boy were unexpectedly caught in a tremendous rainstorm out in the wild. They had spent the afternoon scrambling around fruit trees, and they were about to start back home when the storm began to unleash a torrent of rain. His friend started to scream and cry, trembling with fear. He kept his eyes on the streaks of lightning. Instead of being terrified, he was moved by the extraordinary beauty of the sight. And instead of hiding and taking shelter under a tree like his friend, he struck out walking, challenging the storm. What a downpour, with fiery serpents! What a clamor of terrifying thunder. But after a few minutes, it all stopped. And when, soaked with water and the afterglow of extinct lightning bolts, he went looking for his friend, he found the one who thought himself sheltered and safe, burnt to a char at the foot of the tree...

"It's the cowards who fall. The bullets, like bolts of lightning, chase down the ones who run and hide. Death conquers the one who is afraid of it."

The sweet magnolias continued to open up. The silvery stars continued to open. The wings of love continued to open...

"Have you noticed how this land and this night are like a bride scented with flowers, perfumed with kisses?"

She offered him her lips, a chalice of rose and sorrow, totally submissive in overflowing passion. And it was he who, after kissing her more with his soul than with his lips, now thought of the little rose-colored house, of the lighted altar, of this woman, this virgin, this illusory butterfly that, the instant it goes to sip the honey of the roses, is left pierced and wounded by the spikes of the rose bush.

As he stood up, he was dying:

"Goodbye."

They walked across the garden without speaking until they came to the door.

One more kiss, the final one:

"Goodbye!"

"Goodbye!"

And suddenly she found herself alone, all alone, abandoned among the flowers, in the shadows.

So that she would not fall to the ground, she leaned against the trunk of a tree...

"Nando...! Nando...! My love...!"

She was overcome with sobbing. Little by little she was slipping down unable to hold herself upright any longer, falling to her knees, falling, at last, face down at the foot of the tree...

"Nando..."

The stars wrapped her in their white sendal, and the magnolias perfumed her collapse.

"Nando...!"

He could not hear her, he was far away now, driving the car that seemed to have wings, flying. He drove into the gardens of the house and quickly ran up the stairs. He nearly stumbled over Ramon and Sandoval who were waiting for him impatiently.

"Pepe...! You...?"

"Yes, I came from the estate... Orders. Let's go together..."

"And Papa...? And Natalia...?"

"They're staying back there; they've resigned themselves to it."

He went into his room and came out shortly afterward, holding his saber. A servant carried the bags to the car.

"Shall we go?"

"Let's go!"

He gave his uncle a warm hug:

"Goodbye, Uncle Ramon!"

Don Ramon turned his head aside so that no one could see his tears.

"Goodbye, my boy. Be brave...! And good luck...!"

"Take care of Marta, don't let a day go by without visiting her...! And tell Papa not to worry, I'll be back...! Give Natalia a big kiss... Goodbye, Uncle Ramon...!"

He went down first, leaving Sandoval to say goodbye to his uncle, until he appeared, and they left together.

Don Ramon gave orders to lock the doors and turn off all the lights. Then he went into his room and opened a window that looked out on the sea. At that very moment the sirens went off, and the city was left in darkness. Only the water of the bay seemed to be lighted by the fire of the stars. The darkness was thick, and the silence infinite.

Oh, Manila! Oriental princess whose golden sandals kissed the waves and on whose face the sun shone. What hellish dragon with wings of fire was drawing near you, hidden in mystery and in darkness, to dig its claws into your pearled, lily breast?

Don Ramon passed both hands over his burning forehead. Then he held out his right hand with a clenched fist, threatening the void. And his voice reverberated with the scream of the sirens, with the tolling of the bells, over the whisper of the garden fronds, over the murmur of the mournful waves:

"Beasts!"

Beyond the sea and the clouds, beyond the day and the night, the cunning enemy was sharpening its weapons. It was not the grotesque Samurai this time, with their monster masks and a couple of curved sabers across their bellies, soon to be unsheathed, skilled at cutting off heads! No! It had assimilated the warrior science of America and Europe, it had imitated the best military powers of the world, and at the present moment it was the formidable fortress of steel and destruction on the waters, the needle box of cannons in whose wake cities were flattened, the bird of fire that descended from the clouds, carrying beneath its wings fear, terror, death…

"Beasts!"

It had always been their cherished dream to conquer the Philippines. Their lust was the same as the satyr's sensual frenzy for the beautiful nymph. They stalked it like a kite does a dove. They dreamed of devouring it, of dining and becoming intoxicated on its rich and bountiful blood, like a wolf on a gazelle. And now Japan believed that the moment had arrived to attack it. That is what they were telling Don Ramon, the Philippines: this clashing of bells and the sirens, this funereal darkness that was plummeting from the city over the heart of man like an immense, black banner, falling into pieces.

Robles could not remember having been envious of anything or anyone, until a few moments ago, when he had embraced Fernando and Sandoval. Lucky them! They were full of youth and strength; they were full of enthusiasm and life; they were going to fight like men; they were going to be victorious or die for the country; chosen by fortune; predestined for glory.

Oh, how the old man was belittling himself! Why were those weak feet of his dragging him along? Why didn't his arms have enough strength to brandish a weapon? Why, if his spirit showed itself to be fiery and rearing up like a war-horse, was his poor body faltering, lacking strength and vitality?

Suddenly the sirens stopped and the lights came back on. The electric streetlamps glowed again along the boulevard, and the sea was filled with textural radiance. The outlines of several warships could be seen on the bay, and one could hear, very high and far away, the buzz of airplanes in the sky. Then, down the entire avenue came the rumbling of tanks and artillery, crawling along, followed by thousands upon thousands of soldiers... Among them, perhaps, was Fernando. He would be with them, and he would be passing by now, looking toward the houses, saying farewell to the house, to the gardens, and to uncle Ramon as well...

They were marching along in the distance, and they could only be seen en masse. But some officers stood out in front, and one of them, that one who was tall and straight and who was turning his head now, looked like the captain...

"Hey, Fernando, is that you? May God and the Philippines bless you! And when you come face to face with those..., don't let one of them get away, kill as many as you can! They don't deserve mercy! God didn't give us courage just to throw it away on those beasts...!

V

Way up high, in the bluest part, the first bird of fire appeared. Its wings glittered in the noonday sun like large steel fans. And suddenly it seemed to multiply. There were four, five, many more, easily dominating the airspace, flying together or apart, displaying the red sphere of their flag on the whiteness of their flight and the whiteness of the clouds.

Sirens howled, bells pealed out in the open city, terrified, in shock. People ran roughshod, seeking shelter. And suddenly the air was filled with clouds of smoke, and in the terror of the luminescent morning, the first bombs exploded.

Over what person, over what people, were the birds of death angrily hovering? Against what person, against what people, were they deploying their force and amassing their ire. Manila lay without weapons or soldiers. Airfields and encampments and fortresses had been left empty. Where would such a terrible bombardment end up?

Soon the target of their rage was known. The august Dominican temple, the house of gold of the Philippine people, began to collapse, engulfed in flames. The Japanese pilots pummeled its altars mercilessly. And with indelible marks they recorded on their list of spurious victories a good number of illustrious victims: the saints and angels of the temple.

But while this was something, in reality it was nothing. They had to do more. And after the holy masonry, came the girls' school of Santa Isabel, Santa Rosa, Santa Catalina, and the boys' school of San Juan de Letrán. When the barbarity was finished, in the highest heavens, in the bluest of skies, the steel fans of their wings were disappearing. And the birds of fire became lost in the amber of the clouds, over the sea...

No, these were not the painted birds of mythological legend, those that at the dawn of the empire showed their gods how men and birds should love one another. These were not the ones that placed sweet kisses on the ruby lips of Izanami, nor were they ones that caused Izanagi's knees to bow down upon the golden cloud that served as a cradle for the first Emperor. We were not now in the times of golden legends or fanciful tales. Japan was showing what it truly was. And the tree had to be judged by its fruits.

Don Ramon, running from one part of the house to the other, was giving orders to the servants who, overcome with panic, could barely understand a word he said. Objects of cut glass were falling to pieces from the balconies and verandas. Despite the distance, the bombardment had powerfully shaken the homes in the Ermita. The wind drifted, heavy with emissions of dust and fire. Not very far away, great and thick columns of smoke arose into space.

Hours later, when everything was calmer, Robles let himself slump into a sofa, holding his face in his hands, immersed in painful thoughts...

Poor country. Poor people. Poor Philippines. Now the new Prometheus[74] was chained to the Asiatic rock, while his screams of pain and fear were not able to drive away the horrible vulture that was beginning to eat away at his entrails. The tumult of his chains and the desperate wail of his heart were lost in the emptiness, in the hollow of time and of history.

In vain was the blood spilt by Rizal,[75] in order to shape the dawn of our liberty. In vain was the code of honor drawn up by Mabini, as a legacy of patriotic devotion. In vain the heroic feats of Bonifacio, Luna, Jacinto,[76] of Pilar[77] and so many other immortal soldiers on the fields of battle. In vain the two magnificent civilizations, of Spain and of America, that lavishly adorned the spirit and life of the race. In vain, all the sacrifice, all the love, all the virtue... One dismal night, with the howling of beasts and a sword plunged into the heart of the Philippines, had taken the place of the luminous day. Now war, hunger, pestilence and death were riding triumphantly over our lands. Now the Japanese were here.

Days passed by, filled with anxiety and sadness...

And while our soldiers were desperately fighting against infinitely superior forces on the Bataan[78] front, at the fortress of Corregidor,[79] the same way their ancestors died to hold aloft the flags of liberty, the Japanese troops were slipping into Manila, reducing it to a dung-heap as they passed through.

One day the Robles mansion was invaded by a group of officers and soldiers of the imperial forces. A shop worker served as interpreter. So then, who was the owner of this estate? Have him come here immediately.

Don Ramon offered his explanations. The property owner was gone; he was at his home in the countryside. He was only a guest. How could he help them?

He could do nothing. One of the officers gave him a shove and, followed by his companions, he went into the dining hall and prepared a huge banquet. In the meantime, the soldiers forced open the doors to the garage and brought all the automobiles outside. When the feast was over, the officers began to take off their grimy uniforms, and taking over the house, they threw Don Ramon out into the street, ordering him not to show up there again. Then they took stock of the servants, and each of them went into a room with a maid. Through the elegant bedrooms rang out the screams of the chambermaids being raped, with a clatter of glasses and broken bottles, and the shouting of the conquerors as they joked about the despicable, unfolding act with roars of laughter. Banzai Nippon.[80]

Don Ramon, thrown into the gutter, began to wander around like an automaton. In an instant he seemed to have lost his consciousness as a man. Not thinking, not feeling, not even existing. His shadow stretched across the asphalt which was bathed in sunlight, bent and shivering, an errant specter detached from himself, the only life he has. Dragging himself, more than walking, down the dirty, unruly streets where the soldiers were doing as they pleased, beating and lashing anyone they felt like to posts, he made his way through half the city, aimlessly, not knowing where to go. Until he came across a group of foreigners under full escort, and among them Doctor Kauffman and Professor Anselmi stood out prominently.

Kauffman, with open arms, stopped him:

"Listen, Robles, where are you going like that...? What's happened? What's going on...?"

Only then, confronted by Kauffman's astonishment, did Don Ramon realize that they had thrown him out of his house without a hat, without shoes, wearing pajamas. Clothes, money, jewelry, all of it back there, for the Japanese. The only thing he was carrying was his heart, which could not weep even if it wanted to, because it was enraged and beating with hatred and contempt and disgust. And a cloud from hell, red, red, red, filled his eyes and blinded his sight.

Robles was beginning to explain to Kauffman what had happened, when the Italian musician came up from behind him...

"Per la mare de la Totti dal Monte, mio caro Don Ramon. You Filipinos have been looking for mange to scratch. Now you've got your mange: start scratching! Allegro appassionato!"

Don Ramon clenched his fists and slammed them into the eyes of the fascist:

"You, asshole..."

Kauffman and his cohorts stepped in:

"Gentlemen... Gentlemen..."

Anselmi raised his ringing, melodious voice:

"Repeat that, you repeat that and I'll have you arrested by the Japanese... Per la mare de Titta Rufo... You're an American spy... You and all your relatives are against the Japanese."

A policeman came over to calm things down, and he broke up the group. The foreigners walked away, laughing and talking raucously, masters and lords of the new state of affairs. The evening died away slowly. Attached to a large twilit cloud, the trembling bud of a star was trying to burst into flower.

It was then that Don Ramon began to feel the pangs of hunger and a burning thirst. He had been wandering for hours under the sun whose searing rays seemed to have penetrated into his mind. Now the sun was gone. Now there was no light in the sky. Where to go now? To what destination? Where could he find shelter...?

He thought about his family, and more than anyone about Fernando, his Fernando. He would take revenge... He would carry out justice for them all, his people and the country. At that very moment, he would be killing Japanese.

And while thinking of Fernando, he thought about Marta. And he made his way clumsily toward her home.

The house was in darkness. He had to knock many times before they opened the doors. The entire family, unnerved. Deeply moved, Don Eladio wrapped his arms around him.

The following day, after sleeping like a log through the night, devastated and exhausted, Don Ramon awoke at dawn. He was suffocating in the room with heat and pain. His body was hurting, his soul was hurting. Looking into a mirror, he didn't recognize himself. In a day, he seemed to have aged ten years...

He opened the door and went out to the veranda, aching for air and light. Marta came looking for him there herself, carrying a steaming mug of coffee with cream.

A very good morning to you, Don Ramon. Have some coffee while it's still nice and hot. And settle down and relax: everything will turn out all right because the Lord won't abandon us. He had his family right here, and there was no way they would let him leave until the situation was taken care of. Last night she hadn't had time or a chance to tell him the news. Because she did have news, letters from Fernando had come – God only knows how – into her hands. Everything was going along well. The troops were fighting bravely, and the odds were very good that they could hold out until reinforcements arrived from America. Fernando was writing to her confidently and in very good spirits. It was only that there was a sad note in his last letter. Sandoval had been taken prisoner...

Don Ramon took small sips of coffee as he listened to her. An angelic creature, trusting and innocent. May God hear her words and make them a reality, and save her love.

"When and where did that happen to Sandoval?"

"Fernando only says that he was taken prisoner..."

Ramon sighed:

"At least, poor Natalia stands a fifty-fifty chance of not becoming a widow."

And his mind and heart took flight to the country home. What had happened to them? What had fate done with them? How had Lino, who was such a friend and admirer of these hooligans, arranged things to save their lives and their property? Had they shown him any respect? At least, had they not harmed them?

The reports from the provinces to the capital couldn't be sadder. Magnificent cities like Iliolu, Cebú, Cabanatuan and many more had been completely destroyed. The people living in the majority of the towns, after losing everything, had had to uproot themselves and were scraping by in the mountains. The birds of fire had no respect for civilian populations, and piles of bodies of women, children and old men, ripped open on the mud of the roads and public squares, proclaimed the bloody tragedy. Calling themselves savage eagles, the Japanese bombers sowed death wherever they appeared. And they appeared everywhere. Wherever there were soldiers to annihilate with impunity, and wherever there were villages to terrorize and butcher.

In Manila the Americans and subjects of anti-Axis countries were immediately arrested. And all their property was seized. The historical Fort Santiago was filled from the basement to the ceiling with all kinds of citizens who had been savagely tortured and then shot under the slightest pretext. There was no home, or place, that was not searched or sacked at all hours of day or night. The nation's flag was lowered from its mast before the weeping eyes of the entire nation. And a sort of emergency Philippine government was formed, without a flag, without law, without any authority of its own.

That same morning several military men barged into Don Eladio's home, led by one man who boasted of being able to speak Spanish. According to him, he had lived in Mexico for a number of years. He was an intimate friend of general so-and-so, of general john-doe, of general joe-blow, and of general joe-schmo. They had been great generals once. Now they're a gang of bandits. They declared war on Japan...

"We are mucho thirsty right now."

Don Eladio offered them soft drinks, wine.

"Wine? Wines...? If to have English or American whisky, then, then more bueno."

"Cigars... Cigarettes...?"

"Cigarettes, no more. Okay if to have American..."

They began to drink and smoke, talking up a storm in their own language, with all the people in the house silently congregated about them. From time to time, so that he would not seem impolite, the Spanish speaker addressed Marta:

"In Mexico, the señoritas pretty, pretty. And here too. Right now, no more, you."

Marta was praying silently. Trembling with anguish, she could barely murmur thank you.

"I having in Mexico many friends pretty señoritas. Little tiny, blondies, all same. Big eyes, tiny eyes, big feet, tiny feet, all same. Mucho happy, mucho cuddle, mucho pretty..."

He pointed to Doña Claudia:
"Mamacita of you only?"
"Yes, sir."
"Pretty mamacita. In Mexico mucho pretty mamacita, right away... Before, no more. Right now, bad, ugly, dirty. They no loving Japan right now."

And drinking whisky, he laughed foolishly:
"Señorita Filipino good, love Japan mucho. Little tiny, blondie, all same. Big eyes, tiny eyes, big feet, tiny feet, all same. Then, then, okay. Mucho kodomo-baby, half Japan, half señorita Filipino..."

They suddenly noticed the piano. And all eyes turned to Marta.
"The pretty señorita to sing?"
Marta turned crimson down to the roots of her hair.
"No, sir."
The officer bowed down to her with incomprehensible reverence...
"The pretty señorita to play?"
"Very little, only exercises."
The officer bowed again:
"The pretty señorita allowing us to play and sing little no more right away?"
Marta nodded her head.
The officer bowed again:
"Arigato gozaimazu."[81]

They got up to pound on the piano and bellow out in chorus songs from their own country. The dogs joined the chorus, howling from out in the garden. The poor women's nerves were unstrung. Don Eladio broke out in a cold sweat. Don Ramon's entire body was trembling, and he felt like he was losing his mind.

That's the way they were for an hour, and more. Until they grew tired of the music and the alcohol, and began to take their leave with a series of genuflections and phrases worthy of oriental princes.

Except that on the final step of the stairway, the friend of the Mexican generals, half-embracing Don Eladio, whispered in his ear:

"We, seven. Not to be able to fit in one lone coach by and by... Please to lend his automobile one year, two years no more..."

What was poor Don Eladio going to say, what could he say?

"Yes, sir. Take it."

And so they left in the owner's car, showering them with lavish compliments, waving, smiling...

A U.S. Army tank crosses the destroyed gate of Fort Santiago, a 16th century
Spanish colonial fortress used by the Japanese Army as a prison during the war.
Battle of Manila, February 1945
Source: U.S. Dept. of the Army

PART IV

I

Bataan. Dead of night. Whispers of the jungle crowned by the moon. And in the wind and in the bushes a shower of fireflies like a shower of diamonds.

Far from the front, far from the redoubts, beyond the first lengths of barbed wire, the sleeping sands of the beachhead, and the immense mirror turned toward the moon, toward the stars, the sea. A great silence broken from time to time by the screeching of nocturnal birds and the hiss of reptiles hidden in the undergrowth. The island could be called an oriental princess lying on the tomb of the blue night, under white sidereal veils, upon a bed of stone to which the bougainvillea and the hibiscus lend a crimson border.

Cautiously, warily, a company of Philippine soldiers made its way down a ravine. In front, alone, his heart intoxicated by the beauty of the night and the moon – the moon, first love – went Captain Fernando Robles... His orders were to strike the enemy with an offensive movement that would be supported on several flanks by other companies of infantry and artillery. A solemn composure seemed to envelope them all in the calm that always precedes the worst of storms.

Watching over the intense brightness of the skies that were lighting up silvery threads in the foliage, that were illuminating the jungle like a temple in which a multitude of candles would burn, a shadow like a black flag that was going before them, floated mysteriously. Perhaps it was a shred of night, a last cloud, an enormous, wounded vulture. And why not the trail of death?

The troop went down to a level field that was nearly in the open. Suddenly the first bullets came flying at them.

They had been discovered, and the advanced enemy line began the attack. Robles turned to give orders. Several soldiers bent over as the bullets flew past...

"Who are you saluting, dummies...? The Japanese flag...? Take your positions...! Fire...!"

He stepped to the side and began to fire, using the rifle of one of the first victims. The enemy, vigilant and alert, attacked instead of defending itself. The rifles, the machine guns, the artillery thundered out. All the furor of the battle centered on Robles' men for ten or fifteen minutes or more. Until the Japanese found themselves engaged with the other forces, and the firing at the front began to fade away.

Shortly afterward, they began to draw back, but not without continuing to fight like mad men. They gave up the terrain inch by inch, littering it with dead bodies, flags and broken weapons. Our soldiers, tempered now by the heat of battle and with victory clearly in sight, advanced, covered with laurels of glory. In some lines it was necessary to hold them back. Their rush was too great and their eagerness to fight was beyond limits. And while the enemy scattered, being assaulted, routed, the flags of America and the Philippines were mingled, their colors united in the wind, just as the men from the Philippines and America fused their blood as they died for the same cause and the same ideal. But then the birds of fire rose up, looming in the air over them. And a new battle began, terrifying and unequal. How could they stop the airplanes? How could they escape the curtain of shrapnel that was falling from their open talons onto the frightened, surprised troops? The victory ended in defeat. Now our soldiers were the vanquished under the stench of blood and gunpowder in the ravaged night, in the blue and silver night of moon and flowers.

Nearly all of Robles' men were dead. There were only a few left, defending themselves as well as they could from the hurricane of shells. One of his lieutenants shouted at him in the hellish thunder of the bombardment:

"What do we do, Captain?"

"Carry out our duty! Die!"

"Die...?"

A tear came to the poor lieutenant's eyes. He was very young, still nearly a child. He hadn't lived yet, he hadn't suffered, he hadn't loved. Why die? Why give up dawn, spring, love in an instant? The land was filled with flowers and beautiful women. His youth was full of energy and fire. His ardent, thirsty adolescent lips had barely touched the cup of life overflowing with new, warm wine.

He tried to talk, to say something more that Robles did not understand and was not able to understand, because he had felt a strong blow to his shoulder that made him lurch and fall to the ground, senseless...

Then the battlefield disappeared. In its place there spread an immense garden. In the middle of the garden, a small, white house. And in the little white house, she.

"Marta, is that you...?"

Sweet sounding, light music floated on the same wings on which an aroma of oleanders and lilies drifted. A soft, pearly radiance enveloped everything. In the air tiny points of gold flickered, along with flashes of light. A fantastic and unknown place this was, a place outside the world, far away from men.

The figure of a woman, upright and pale, came toward him like a moonbeam, tripping through the flowers, illuminating the entire path with her feet. She came forward like a shining sword, like a burning lance, like an arrow dripping with light.

"Is that you, Marta...?"

The little house, off in the distance, became filled, little by little, with singing and light. The white figure, the pale woman, was now next to the captain. Bending over him as he lay stretched out on a bed of moist, soft grass, she kissed him with her musical voice:

"Nando...! My love...!"

Yes, it was Marta! Her voice like a lyre, her aroma of flowers. Or was it her painful and pure soul, kneeling before the wounded man like a mother at the foot of a cradle. She was coming for him, for his love and for his life, to exchange that bed of roses for the bed of her bosom, of her arms. And he let himself be carried with no will of his own, weak and trembling with love, to the little white house of alabaster lamps and the melody of enchanted epithalamia. He let himself be carried like a child at his mother's breast, like an offering in the hands of a fairy, like a flag on the shoulders of the fatherland...

And now Fernando Robles saw no more, felt no more.

The night passed by.

The moon passed by.

Death passed by with the moon and the night.

But because he loved deliriously and was loved deliriously, the captain could not die.

When many hours later he opened his eyes blinded by the bright afternoon light, he found himself in an emergency field hospital, surrounded by a number of doctors and enemy officers. Without him being aware or even feeling it, they had administered first aid. Some large bandages wrapped around his aching flesh; a feverish weakness kept him on his back; an intense anguish seemed to be thrashing him in the emptiness. And a wrenching, horrible thirst that was making him delirious.

He barely had the strength to lean his head a little when he heard the noise two soldiers were making as they carried past him the dead body of his lieutenant. They had not been able to save him. How could they save him if he had his chest ripped open by shrapnel?

He gave in, protesting, before death, a romantic youth whose unfortunate parents would weep for their entire lives, along with a grateful country.

But what was the anguish of some parents and the fervor of the country, compared to the joy of life, of living to the full, intoxicated with dawns, springs, loves, in a land that the poor fellow could dream of, full of flowers and beautiful women?

Poor lieutenant! And like him, how many other boys have fallen and continue to fall because of their belief in democracy, their devotion to liberty and their love for the land where they were born. The flower of youth, born to be sacrificed, a phalanx of idealistic volunteers, with the marrow of heroes and the heart of eagles.

Many of them would embark on a romantic adventure, with fanatical eagerness, while opportunity smiled down upon them, and death, like a sweetheart veiled in immaculate gauze, awaited them impatiently, anxiously. Now the great lady could be satisfied. She was getting her fill of lovers at every hour. The troubadours of illusions, the lovers of glory were forming pyres of bloody, broken flesh at her feet.

After being bedridden for several weeks, owing more to the loss of blood than the seriousness of the wound, Fernando Robles was put in a concentration camp, marking another number in the already alarming list of official prisoners. He had to tell friends his name before they could recognize him. Then, sickly, pale, his hair and beard grown out, no one would even guess that he was the same handsome, dashing young man they had been with not so long ago. He looked like a ghost of his former self; the caricature of a man; the reality of war.

The days and nights slid by for him with the lethargy of centuries, with the monotony of a cruel nightmare. He scarcely ate, his sleeping was worse, and if it were not for the force of his spirit, and the reserve energy of his youth, he would have died of dejection and misery, physically incapable of withstanding the weight of such a heavy burden.

But he shouldn't, he couldn't, he did not want to stop living. A blessed memory, a beautiful chimera of dazzling wings floated before his eyes, guiding him toward a better future. Because of this chimera and because of his memory, he did not feel the stones that wounded his feet, or the thorns that pierced his flesh along the road. Take up your cross and follow me, said the Divine Redeemer. He walked with the cross on his back, following the Son of God along the cruel road. At the end of this road, high up on Calvary, a woman was waiting to kiss his lesions and wash his wounds with her tears.

Everything was done well, everything was brought into service as it should have been. When his father predicted this disaster, he was wrong. Because this was not being quixotic, this was called selflessness. Nor was it suffering, it was immortality. And he, Fernando Robles, had not fought, nor was he suffering for America, for the Philippines, or any other country in particular. He had thrown himself into battle for the happiness of all people, for the freedom of the world, with God in his heart and the name of love on his lips.

The name of his love! Marta! Five letters of light that were all the light in the sky and on earth! Now he recalled vaguely how he saw her in a feverish moment when he fell, wounded. How she was next to him, kissing his blood, and fighting away his dying. How, to avoid enemy fire, she had carried him to the little white house...

He was caressing her rosary in his hands when a Japanese guard noticed it:

"What is that...? Give me that gold bracelet."

Fernando became alarmed:

"It's not a bracelet, it's a rosary. We use it when we pray."

The other man approached him irritably:

"No matter what it is; hand it over."

"I can't give it to you, it isn't mine."

"I don't care whose it is."

"No."

He felt a blow to his chest and fell at the guard's feet. When he recovered, he no longer had the rosary in his hands. They had taken it from him. They had stolen it.

His keepsake! His talisman! The one she had given him, wet with her tears and kisses on that unforgettable night when he went away. Something that was a part of her and a part of heaven. Each bead on the blessed rosary, a teardrop from her eyes. And her heart and her cross, her own heart and her own cross!

It seemed to him that he had lost her forever, all alone now, helpless, he had allowed that yellow beast to stab her, right before his eyes. He felt like the sun had sunk into the bowels of the earth, and that the world had suddenly come undone. It seemed like God, the good God, was abandoning him...

That night he prayed, counting the Hail Marys on his fingers. And for all of the nights that followed, he cried like a baby. And so the days went, passing, passing by, long, sad, filled with melancholy and despair.

But as time went on, the conditions for the prisoners gradually improved. One day they were allowed to write and receive letters. On another day, they had visitors. On yet another day, they released the weakest and sickest ones.

They were no longer enemies, they were friends, working together to form a new, larger Asia. Japan could only see every dark-skinned man as an ally against the yoke, the despotism and the exploitation of England and America. Indians and Malaysians became Asiatic, beyond the rhythm of their blood and geographical laws, due to the delirium of greatness of the divine yellow puppet that millions of idolatrous suicides worshipped on bended knees. And all things were becoming Asia.

Fernando took advantage of the situation to write to Marta and to his father. If they even knew that he was still alive! But time continued to pass by unvaryingly. Day after day, with maddening slowness, and the letters he was waiting for did not arrive. Even through the prisoners' wire fencing where his companions could be seen with their relatives, no matter how he wore out his eyes, he did not see one familiar face.

With the visits of strangers to the camp there came news from everywhere, and the air was filled with rumors. The depravities committed by the invading army became known. They mulled over the affronts, the grief and the ruin of thousands upon thousands of innocents, barbarously martyred to the lust, to the criminal pillaging of the conquerors. Brothers? Allies? Men of the same race? Never! Filipinos were not descendants of Asiatic pirates. Their ancestors were not savage warriors of female slaves and a hypocritical cult to the shadows of the dead and the image of death. The blood running through our veins was not yellow like pus and bile, but red, red, the blood of men, the blood of a people, the blood of God.

It might well be that some ill-advised, ignorant Filipinos of unruly disposition and low morals could go along with their theories and share their false beliefs. It might well be that parties of faint-hearted men and women of a servile nature could form in favor of that deceptive propaganda. And it might even be that there are poor in spirit who would see high honors and divine blessings in the zeal to turn the Philippines into cannon fodder. All that could well be. Because there is no religion without its apostates, nor any paradises without their serpents, and because in every group of people, as in every flock, there graze black sheep.

But those groups, those parties, that horde of abject fools, do not make up the Philippine people, they do not inspire the Philippine soul, they could not be the race that knelt to the true God, passed their own laws and raised their beloved flag, respected by all nations.

No, the Japanese had not come to give us freedom, of which we have more than enough, or to give us anything except hunger, destruction and death. Quite the opposite: instead of giving, they took everything. And in doing this, they turned out to have an even more horrifying voracity than locusts, for when these fell upon a plantation, they left the roots intact. The Japanese did not leave even the roots. They devoured everything.

One day Fernando saw the guard who had robbed him of Marta's rosary. He saluted him, smiling. Then Fernando approached him:

"Do you still have that bracelet?"

"Yes."

"Do you want to trade it to me for a watch that is even more valuable?"

"Where is the watch?"

It was magnificent, gold, with his initials engraved on the back plate, studded with precious stones.

The Japanese opened wide his eyes, his mouth, his arms...

"Oooooh...!"

He couldn't believe there existed such a treasure. In his country, that was worth a geisha, one's life. His hands trembled as he took the jewel, making it quickly disappear into his pocket.

All right. A done deal. He would go and get the bracelet right away. Just wait for a minute, just a few minutes...

And Fernando waited in vain. He never saw him again.

III

Don Lino spent the night dreaming that a mischievous little boy was riding on his knees which had become a spirited steed...

"Sonny...! Sonny...!"

Where did that child want to go? To greet the princess who was asleep in her palace in Arayat?[82] To surprise the gnomes hiding among the trunks of the tamarinds? Or would he rather chase butterflies of ivory and gold over the corollas of daisies...?

Bah! The child wasn't interested in dragonflies, or in sylphs, and not even in the beautiful Sleeping Princess. He held his little hands out toward the river, the bright, clear river of the estate, where tiny, silvery fish were leaping under the open bills of the herons.

"Sonny...! Sonny...!"

So then, they were going to the river. The little fellow was the king of the world, and Don Lino was his most submissive vassal. In addition to the little fish and the enormous birds, the river, with its watery laces, watched over the nymphs with their eyes of pearls and their green tresses of the finest jades.

"Sonny...! Sonny...!"

They were going to the river! The spirited steed was galloping so swiftly that it seemed as though each hoof was sprouting wings...! A little further and they would reach the bubbling current.

He woke up, shaken, enmeshed between his sheets and the light of dawn, for the roosters were crowing, poets of daybreak. And his first thought, as he awoke, was for his daughter. Because wasn't that, perhaps, the child they were waiting for? He would tell her his dream. If she could have seen the little one! The most beautiful creature in the world!

He went down to the garden, leaving behind the mansion, asleep and silent. In the distance, under the bright sky, the top of Arayat appeared momentarily between the clouds that enveloped it at night like a veil embroidered with stars. At its feet, stalks could be seen waving slightly, golden and magnificent, like swords in the wind. And little by little, under the mist, torn by the darts of a rising sun, the frizzy nipa palms of the vast hamlet became highlighted.

The estate was waking up. The land was becoming filled with whispers and murmurs of life. Except that Don Lino began to be bewildered at not seeing people anywhere. Where were the people from his fields? Into what cloud had they evaporated?

As if responding to his bewilderment, in the empty space of the path a human figure suddenly appeared. But instead of walking, it was rushing toward him. Don Lino adjusted his glasses to see better, and discovered Father Elías running, his cassock wrapped around his waist. What had gotten under that blessed priest's skin so early in the morning? Had they stolen his candleholders? Did the bell tower collapse?

He finally arrived, panting, wiping away the sweat running down his face with a huge handkerchief. And he spoke breathlessly:

"News – awful, miserable, terrible news, dear sir! The Japanese invaded the town last night. They were moving closer now, coming right behind him, they were right on his heels...

"Get ready, sir. They are very wicked. They've done horrible things in town..."

Don Lino smiled pitifully at the priest:

"Don't worry. They won't do anything to us. I know them. I know how to deal with them..."

"Look..."

"It's nothing. What you need is a good breakfast to perk you up physically and morally. After you've gobbled down a good helping of ham and eggs, along with a heaping cup of cocoa, sursum corda!"[83]

And they were eating breakfast when they heard rifle shots and shouting in the gardens.

Don Lino stood up:

"Don't be frightened... Everyone quiet... I'm going out to meet them... These people aren't barbarians like the whites... These people are super-civilized..."

In only a few minutes these "super-civilized" men stormed in and took over the breakfast table, and made the owners themselves serve them everything they had. After they had their fill of eating and drinking, they began to search and sack the house. In the meantime, downstairs, they took the cars and barrels of essentials from the garages...

Don Lino began to protest in indignation:

"But listen, listen, we are Filipinos, farmers, peaceful people, friends..."

The officer in command of the squad looked at him over his shoulder contemptuously:

"The imperial army needs everything we are taking. Do you have anything more to say?"

Yes, he had more to say, a lot more. He had to spit in their faces with words of his own language, telling them that they were a bunch of uniformed bandits and thieves. Except that he suddenly felt that he had no words, that there was no floor beneath him, and that the entire house was collapsing on his old body, as he listened in horror to the shouts of terror and desperation of Natalia, shut up inside her room by a group of soldiers...

"Father...! Father...!"

Like a wounded beast he threw himself at the door which was locked tight from the inside. And he began to pound it with his fists, with his feet, with his head. It was useless! The door did not give way, no matter how hard the old man drove himself with the incredible force of his nerves and his spirit. And he was alone, entirely alone, with no one able to help him, while more weakly, more hushed at moments, the sad voice crying out for help, continued to bore into his ears and his heart:

"Father...! father...! father...!"

When the doorway was finally opened, the heroes of the imperial army who were coming out, had to go by, stepping on the inert body of Don Lino. In the room, they left a corpse. Natalia, her entire body and her clothing, torn apart, soaking in blood...

But what did that matter to them? Over there, in their beautiful country of legend and poetry, where even reptiles are sacred, and it is a crime to pluck the petals from a flower; where stones are venerated and the moss is caressed; where the laws of honor are set above the laws of life, life and a woman's honor are worth much less than a paper fan.

They had taken away Father Elías right at the beginning so that he would hand over the bells and any metal items in the church. When he refused to give them the chalice, they pummeled him. When he managed to recover, he quickly went to the manor house. The Japanese had left now, and everything was calm again. By then the sun was moving past the rim of the heavens, unfolding its golden banners to the wind.

He found Don Lino, face down, over the dead body of his daughter. And he slumped to his knees, blind with grief and terror, his arms held out in the form of a cross and his eyes lost on high:

"Lord...! Lord...!"

How long did the old priest stay there, praying before the tragic ensemble of the lifeless woman and the poor old man fallen over her like a tree shattered by lightning? Voices of some of the servants coming back to the house pulled him out of his enervation. And he saw how Don Lino began to recover, little by little, sitting up, then jumping to his feet...

"Where are the Japanese?"

His voice sounded hoarse and terrible, rumbling through the house like thunder. His eyes were flecked with blood, and his entire body was soaked with sweat; he was trembling, racked by the coldness of death. Faced by the silence that his shouting caused, he clutched the arms of Father Elías.

"Why don't you answer me, damn you? Who do you think is talking to you? Tell me where those bastards are!"

Crestfallen, the priest understood. And he again opened his arms and raised his eyes to pray:

"Lord...! Lord...!"

The old man, Robles, had lost his mind. Carefully and tenderly, Father Elías tried in vain to comfort him, to bring him back to reality. Don Lino began to rave, to laugh, to go all through the house, shouting, until finally he fell into an armchair, sobbing desperately...

Then the priest ordered a servant-girl to wrap Natalia's body in a shroud. They would bury her as quickly as possible. In the meantime, the other servants watched Don Lino carefully, as he continued to show signs of sudden dementia. Hours later he seemed to be asleep with his eyes wide-open, his mouth slack, sunken into the plush chair, as the day sweetly passed in a magical sheen of colors, the birds returned to their nests in the foliage, and the Arayat, like a monk wearing a grey sackcloth over his head, wrapped its tip with the throbbing shadows of dusk. They placed Natalia's body, sheathed in a snow-white shroud of cloth and flowers, on a stretcher made of reeds, at the road to the small cemetery of the property. Behind the body which was carried by some servants, walked Father Elías with a wooden cross over his shoulder. He walked along praying and stumbling over every stone, over every bush, that he seemed not to notice. Oh, vanity of human things...! Our Father Who art in heaven...! Oh, mysterious designs of the Almighty...! Hallowed be Thy name...! Who would have ever dared think that this would be the end of these people, so privileged and honored, of this kind of princess, ravished, murdered by a mob of criminals, and that poor, unfortunate man, so respected and powerful only hours before, now despairing, lost in a corner of his palatial dwelling, moaning in horrible anguish, the most miserable of men...

They arrived at the rustic cemetery. They dug a grave. They set Natalia's remains in it; they covered it with earth. And Father Elías blessed the ground in the name of the Father, in the name of the Son and the Holy Spirit...

"Deus cuius miseratione animae fidelium requiescunt, hune tumulum bendicere dignare, sique Angelum tuum sanctum deputa custodent; et quorus quorumque corpora hic sepelientur, animas quorum ab omnibus absolve vinculis directorus, ut in te semper cum Sanctis tuis sine fine detentur. Per Christum Dominum nostrum. Amen."

Night now, pleasant oriental night crowned with light and perfumed with herbs and flowers from the jungle, when Father Elías slowly, sadly, returned to the Robles mansion. He walked alone, with only his sorrowful thoughts for company. He had planted the cross on Natalia's grave. His companions had been quick to melt away...

He was stopped by a shout when he reached a bend in the road.

"Halt!"

And a man wielding a revolver emerged from the bushes...

"Halt!"

The priest stopped. The man stepped out resolutely.

"Don't be frightened, Father. It's me, Pablo, the foreman of the ranch. Where are you going?"

"To the manor house to see Don Lino: he's sick, he's delirious..."

"It's useless, don't go on. Don Lino isn't in the house; he's run off, and nobody knows where he is. They've been going after him and looking for him, with no success. It's like the jungle has swallowed him up."

Father Elías shuddered:

"This too... Good Lord!" Then he said to the man:

"All right. And you, Pablo, what do you want? Why did you stop me?"

The foreman straightened up:

"To tell you to come with us."

"With you? Who...? And where?"

"With us, with all the people from the ranch. There are hundreds of us, and there are going to be thousands. We're going into the hills, to make up bands of guerrillas, to kill, to die. Those pigs have torn apart our homes, they've raped our women, tortured our men, butchered entire towns, down to the last person. They imagine that we're afraid of them! They thought when they saw us whipped that we had gone down on our knees to them! The bastards...! Now they'll see, when the time is ripe, just who we Filipinos are!"

The priest held his arms out to the man's face:

"Pablo, Pablo, remember the divine law: Thou shalt not kill!"

Then the man roared right back at him:

"Then is it forbidden to kill rapid dogs, or poisonous snakes?"

"The Japanese are human beings..."

"The Japanese are swine filled with devils that the Holy Bible talks about! Do you think I don't know any Latin? You've come to us so many times, preaching about these things."

Father Elías restrained himself and was silent, he relaxed his ashen brow. Why quarrel? Why argue? Before him was a man whose mind was made up, who was desperate, capable of anything. When he turned around after a brief pause, he found himself surrounded by farmhands armed with rifles and bolo knives. A voice tore through the silence:

"All right. What, then? We can't stay here all night. Is the Father coming with us or not?"

"I can't follow you. My holy orders won't allow me. Don't forget that a priest is above men, that I am only an old, humble servant of God, and also, in the name of God, I condemn and rebuke your behavior!..."

Voices cried out in protest:

"What...?"

"Become peaceful again, give in to order, learn to suffer, resign yourselves to being patient. It is by the will of the Almighty that these things are happening. Trust in God, have faith in His divine mercy, be good, pray, lift your hearts to heaven..."

"Padre...!" shouted Pablo, interrupting him. "We're not here to listen to sermons...! Either come with us or...!"

"Or what...?"

The foreman walked away, turning his back. Then he shouted an order:

"Tie him to a tree, and let the ants eat him there. If we let him go free, he'll sell us out. Priest and all! Good words and bad intentions."

The old priest sobbed:

"In the name of God, what are you saying? What do you plan to do, you poor soul?"

He didn't hear him. He had gone away quickly, leading the men around him. Only two were left behind, tasked with tying up the priest. But instead, they let him go free, with his word that he would run away, go into hiding, disappear from sight.

Dragging himself along, more than walking, he tried to reach the house, lost in the pitch dark of the night. Until suddenly an immense blaze rose up before him, a tongue of fire, high and straight, that lit up the skies, blotting out the flickering stars, shrouded in dense red, gray and blue smoke... The house was burning on all four sides, burning up entirely like a gigantic torch, burning mercilessly and without love, perhaps to erase all traces of pain and crime.

Why go on toward something that was ceasing to exist? A hot wind, full of sparks, lashed out at the old priest. A wall of flames, growing higher and higher, stopped him on the road. He went back along the path he had traveled, turning his back to the sinister, fierce dragon of smoke and fire that came on, roaring and devouring everything in its path. Finally, he reached the little house that served him as a monastery, where he collapsed on a rickety bed until dawn, when some women urgently called out for his presence.

They had found the corpse of Don Lino on the flowery riverbank of his great estate.

III

A few days after they occupied the Philippines, the Japanese civil component multiplied throughout the country in a miraculous way.

They came through the air, over the sea, from the clouds and the waves, in such swarms that they darkened space. And they were the masters and lords of this dreamed of paradise. Now the public and private enterprises that they would spread themselves over were theirs. First of all, the press.

"La Linterna" passed into the hands of their editors. And then began the cynical and ridiculous, mendacious and violent propaganda against everything that did not smell one-hundred percent Japanese. The Japanese civilians turned out to be more arrogant and despicable, whenever and wherever they appeared, than even the military. They were the informers, the spies, the ones dedicated to the most abominable offices and the vilest duties. They transformed the press into a garbage heap, turning Filipino journalists into an instrument of their machinations.

They raised that poor devil Andrade to the position of editor in chief of "La Linterna." And Andrade, feeling more like a Japanese than Tokyo, immediately set himself to praising in every fashion and through all means the fantastic glories of the greatest oriental Asia. He began to eat in public, sitting on his haunches; he gave up cutlery in favor of Asian chopsticks; he learned to speak broken "Nipponese" with an old Japanese hetaira; and without prejudice to lick the heels of the new Filipino governors; in the most prominent place of his home he built a Shinto[84] altar, along with its accessories, to worship the Mikado. He wasn't satisfied with publishing libels in the newspaper. He went wandering all around the city preaching, by word and example, the love, the fervor and gratitude that the Philippine people owed to their bow-legged conquerors. From his watchtower he insulted those who would not share his fondness of the Japanese. And for everything, he made use of the money of the Japanese and the packed wallets of some gullible and fearful Filipinos who knew he was all-powerful in the new order of things, and let themselves be swindled openly and of their own free will.

This was living, this was life, and not that poor, miserable life of the past. This was what it was like to be an important man and talk like a fancy-pants on a pulpit bristling with bayonets, without being afraid that anyone would dare criticize the daily heap of drivel that mucked up the paper he was in charge of. And to live to see it, sir. All those people who had run away from his greetings and his scrounging before, were now his best friends and his most obsequious admirers. Oh, no. He examined his conscience every day. He was not a bad man. He was just a rascal, that's all.

The poor fellow just frightened people. He and the bunch of scribblers and reporters he had under him. Luckily for their hide, the general public didn't take them seriously. People paid as much attention to them as the moon does to barking dogs. Too bad for heroic propaganda! Too bad for the amorous serenades to the greatest oriental Asia! What a waste of paper and ink!

One fine day "La Linterna" awoke ringing all the bells and blowing all the whistles. Japan was preparing to give the Philippines their independence. Oh, what a great, generous heart! Oh, that blessed, praise-worthy nation! America never wanted to do that! Spain never thought of doing that! Now we had a republic, salvation, freedom!

But, oh, it was just that the Japanese in the country kept multiplying, to guard it and defend it against the Americans, just in case they got a notion to come back in spring like the dark swallows. And to make a show of such a highly noble decision, they gave the Philippines their freedom with music. A certain Yamada,[85] an illustrious flutist, considered to be the Wagner of Japan, would make a very special journey from Kobe to beguile the Philippine government and its people.

Along with the country, art would be redeemed. All the native music-makers, their heads bowed down before the magical baton of Yamada, would begin to be musicians. And to be patriots. Because what other sort of patriotism can compare to Japanese patriotism? And what other kind of harmony can compare to Japanese harmony? When Bonaparte got it into his head to say that the worst noise of all was music, it was because the poor fellow had never heard the sweet sound of the "shamisen" accompanied by a "geisha's" mewing to the moon, or the bellowing of a fervent Buddhist monk throwing incense at a Buddha's bellybutton.

In the meanwhile, hunger was beginning to hover sinisterly and frighteningly, like a gigantic vulture, covering cities and towns with its menacing shadow. There was no rice, there was no sugar, there was no corn, no legumes, no potatoes, nothing... Where was all that? Did the rats destroy it? Did the locusts eat it all? Tokyo needed to provide the answers!

Hunger became the always divine inspiration for geniuses. Perhaps this was why, in pursuit of Asiatic worship, there unexpectedly arose a fluster of poetasters, litterateurs, orators, music-makers, songsters and suffragettes who thundered and stormed in the press, in the theater, in the music houses, and on radio stations. It was a matter of reasoning it out. And eating. Especially eating. Give me rice and call me a Japanese dog!

Overnight, dark, young ladies and many who were quite white, spume of the lowest social tides, became known as "geishas". And from them, bordellos and clinics for contagious diseases reaped their benefits. Unspeakable spiritual and carnal putrefaction. If these wretched creatures went on calling themselves Philippine women, it would be a matter of ripping the blessed name of the country to pieces.

One morning, the sad, grief-stricken figure of an old man appeared before the dictatorial desk of Andrade...

"Mister director of 'La Linterna'?"

"That's me. What do you want?"

"I am Ramon Robles. I've come to ask if you would like to..."

Andrade got to his feet. Then he bowed for some time and began to stammer:

"Robles...! Damn! Robles! Robles, the millionaire..."

"Just Ramon Robles, that's all. I've come here because I don't know where else to go, to find out what has happened to my nephew. He was released some time ago, a long while back, but the fact is, nobody knows where he is, he's disappeared. Maybe, since you're a friend of Fernando and a journalist, you might have some news. Do you know what's become of him? Do you know where I can find him?"

Andrade shook his head, no:

"I don't know anything about your nephew, Mr. Robles. I don't know a thing, but I can find out. Please have a seat."

He pointed to a chair in front of his desk. Don Ramon let himself fall wearily, weakly, appreciative and thanking Andrade's interest from the bottom of his heart, while the journalist was speculating from the very beginning about a good business deal that he could exploit, as he contacted various official departments on the telephone. When he was finished talking, he adopted a grave and mysterious air. Suddenly he asked:

"Was he in Tarlac?"

"Yes, sir."

"His ranch, his home, is in Tarlac, isn't it?"

"It was. Now it's all just a pile of ruins. No house, no ranch, nothing."

"And the workers you had?"

"In the hills."

Andrade thought it was his duty to pound on the desk...

"Carrying out guerrilla warfare, huh?"

Don Ramon looked at the desk sympathetically, and shrugged:

"God only knows!"

As though to put an end to the interview, Andrade got to his feet again:

"Look, Mr. Robles, I could help you find out where your nephew is. But to do it, I would have to use certain means that I can't tell you about. Are you willing to spend a bit of money? Because you'll have to come up with some money..."

"How much?"

"Not a lot; five or six thousand pesos."

Don Ramon did not hesitate:
"You'll tell me if your efforts have any success?"
"I guarantee it."
"In that case, please hand me a pen..."
He held out a check and gave it to the illustrious director of "La Linterna."
"When do you think I should come back to find out from you...?"
Andrade hastily replied, as he put the check in his wallet:
"No, don't bother coming back here... That's not advisable... It's a very delicate matter... Give me your address... I'll go there myself, and let you know."

He stayed there, rubbing his hands together, as Don Ramon walked away. Some days are truly a blessing. And it's not just one idiot, it's a dozen idiots who are born every minute, every day. He sat down in front of the Remington, and typed out with a fictitious date:

"My dear Mr. Robles:
Pardon me for not going to see you personally as we agreed. It isn't wise. The gentleman we are interested in is in the hills at the present time, with his people. The reports that I have are reliable, as I have spared no expense in obtaining them. With the deep appreciation I have for all of you, I am truly sorry for what is happening.
Yours, with the greatest respect,
A."

And that was that. He would send the letter within the week. In six minutes he had made six-thousand pesos. Oh, magnificent Asia! You were never greater for the famous Andrade than you were today!

In the meantime, hesitantly and slowly, Don Ramon walked away from the offices of the great newspaper. He was thinking about the strange behavior of the director of "La Linterna." Was it possible that he was a charlatan? Could it turn out that he was a swindler who would hold onto the cash himself, and make up fictional tales? Anyway, what did money matter? Not just a fistful of thousands: the poor old man would give his entire fortune without a second thought if he could find out where Fernando was, what had become of Fernando, dead or alive!

They were the only two members of the family left in the world. That blessed Lino, so optimistic, such a dreamer, dead: the sad, romantic victim of his crazy ideas and his false ideals. Poor Natalia, dead, murdered so shamefully, so horribly. And Doctor Sandoval, dead too, while he was doing his duty in a bloodied hospital, bombed by the Japanese.

He had promised Marta that he wouldn't rest until he found out about Fernando. And he would find out. He would know, sooner or later. He hung onto hope from his dealings with Andrade. If Andrade's inquiries failed, where could he go then? But Andrade wasn't going to fail. His old heart told him so. Unless the earth had opened up to bury the brave Captain in its very abysses...

The earth had not opened up. Late into the festive night of stars and music of breezes and flowers, the Captain was working his way cautiously and furtively into the garden of his beloved. There was one lone light in the house, the blue porcelain globe in Marta's bedroom. Through an open window, between the wrought iron bars of the grate, the gentle glow splashed onto the sweet roses of a climbing rosebush. Fernando looked through the roses. On her knees, before an image of the Virgin, she was praying with her hands together, the same way angels prayed, with their wings folded.

Silence. Everything was silent and asleep, except for that poor prostrate girl, and the Captain's heart that was crying out in unbounded grief as he savagely pounded his chest:

"Goodbye, Marta, goodbye! I'm going to die!"

Yes, he was going to die. Now he had decided to sacrifice his life, once and for all. He had already offered it, already risked it for the country, for glory, for freedom. And he was standing. He was free of his wounds and his illness, for this, in the end to give up the love of loves of his Marta, who was the only reason for living, for this life that he had sworn to sacrifice now, before the shadows of his dead ones, over the blood of his father and of his sister.

He looked at his beloved, trembling with passion, with feverish, mad eyes, caressing – because he was not able to caress her – the petals and thorns of the roses. Impossible to leave in any other way. If she knew the truth, the poor girl would die first, or he would completely lose his courage, and renounce his sacred oath.

He kissed the bars of the grate, he kissed the roses, he even kissed the ground of the garden. And afterward he fled, like a desperate man, losing himself in the festive night of stars and music of breezes and flowers.

IV

A month went by. Many months went by, while Fernando did not realize how quickly time was flying, and it was flying like a bird, not leaving a trace in the air or in his life. The master and lord of the hills, fearsome knight-errant of the forests, his followers went with him everywhere there were Japanese to kill. They made up a small army of more than a thousand determined and brave men. Their bellicose actions would fill more than a glorious page in our history.

They killed the Japanese as boldly as they had killed the insects that attacked the fields not long ago, or the serpents that coiled around at their feet. And on the nights when he came back weary, after battling for hours and hours, Fernando rested peacefully, a child asleep in the soft bosom of night, to the murmurs of the forest's song, feeling on his closed eyelids the sweet caress of the kisses of flowers and nacre from the moon.

In the rustic hut under a canopy of palms that he used for shelter and housing, the Captain was taking a nap when several soldiers came up to him, dragging along an enemy prisoner.

They had hunted him down like a deer while he was daringly going into a thicket with a pair of companions. The latter two were now keeping company with the shades of their ancestors. The one they were bringing as a prisoner had surrendered when he found himself alone and lost. Seeing that he was before the head of that troop, he stood at attention and saluted with a bloody arm.

He spoke Tagalog,[86] and made himself understood perfectly. Without knowing why, Fernando became interested in him:

"Are you wounded?"

"It's nothing, sir. Just a scratch. It's not even close to my heart..."

The Captain smiled:

"Are you a spy?"

"No, sir; I'm a soldier."

"What were you and your friends doing in the hills? Weren't you even aware that we were around here?"

"Absolutely, sir. Our own troops aren't far away. My buddies and I have been lost in the jungle since yesterday. We were looking for orchids, wild chickens, fruit... This is all so beautiful, this golden mountaintop, this green temple of birds and sunshine...!"

The Captain sat up in his hammock:

"You're too well spoken to be just a simple soldier. Tell me, why did you surrender instead of die fighting like your companions? Don't you people crow about wanting to die before you'll surrender? You're my prisoner of war. Before I have you shot, explain yourself."

The yellow man bowed his head and began to talk timidly and ashamed.

He had surrendered because he loved life. He was only one of hundreds of thousands of soldiers of his race who had been forced to fight for the Emperor with heroic words on their lips, while nursing a great, sad cowardice a the bottom of their heart. The Captain seemed like a good man, and he would tell him the truth before he died. Back in Nagoya he had a humble little paper house. His old mother cried for him every night when she lit the lamp at home. His young wife offered up to him, on the family altar, a spray of flowers and a glass of wine every day. And his two little ones, a boy and a girl, were always asking at all hours: "When is my papa coming home?" They waited for him at the gate, by the side of the road, at all hours. Like no one else, and more than anyone else, these beloved ones needed his courage and his life. He was not a coward, no. He wasn't afraid of death. What he dreaded deeply, bitterly, was leaving those poor pieces of his soul alone and abandoned.

"Especially my children, so small, so weak…"

Besides, he didn't think of the Filipinos as his enemies. Why should they kill him? Japan had just given the Philippines their independence. As a Japanese and as a soldier, he couldn't understand this suicidal, fratricidal fight between the guerrillas and the imperial forces…

Then it was Fernando who made him be quiet, speaking loudly and forcefully:

"If there was one man in the whole world, one Philippine heart, noble and honorable, who loved and defended your country more fervently, that Philippine soul, that man, was my father, the powerful lord and master of this entire place. He died, insane with grief and fear, his heart broken when he saw his pregnant daughter raped and murdered by your companions, Japanese soldiers, when they attacked our property to sack it and destroy it. What you have done to us, you have done to everyone else. My country welcomed you, trusting and resigned, with the white flag of peace in its arms. You shoved it down, so that it would fall to its knees before your dirty boots. And you tortured it, you wounded it, you stomped all over it, soaking it in blood and fire. You know how to plead for your home and your loved ones, you pig! Turn around and look at the hundreds of thousands of men like you, who have lost their loved ones and their homes without being your enemies, for the mere crime of being Filipinos, on the altar of your homicidal fury, innocent victims of your barbarity and the criminal law of your might. And what liberty do you dare talk about that Japan could possibly give us if, when you attacked, the Philippines was freer than ever, and freer than Japan can possibly be?"

He was suddenly silent, as if to catch his breath from the fire of his words and the bitterness of his memories. And then Pablo came up, absorbed and in a hurry, to tell him that Father Elías had just arrived and was looking for him.

Before he could recover from his astonishment at this visit, the broken figure of the priest, dressed like a farmer and armed with a reed cane, appeared before him, humble, smiling, serene...

"My dear sir, Don Fernando... My dear Mr. Captain...!"

Fernando was taken aback:

"Just a minute, Padre!"

He called out to Pablo and gave him orders. They were to confine the Japanese soldier, attend to his wounds, give him something to eat if he was hungry, not mistreat him... Then, turning back to the priest:

"Now I'm at your disposal, Padre. But first you have to tell me how you were able to get here, and especially, what is it that brought you here?"

"I've followed the goats' paths, guided by love, in the name of our Lord, Jesus Christ!"

Stop, Father Elías. He couldn't listen to him, or help him in any way. If he was going to start talking like that, he knew where it was likely to end up. They had misled him, he was fooling himself if he thought that he would give up his mission, his duty, for anything or anyone. If not even his love for Marta, which was his very own life, wasn't enough to stop him... what power, what force, what hell could stop him?

"Love, Captain, sir."

Fernando shouted, his anger suddenly mounting. But wasn't he telling him that he had given up love? What sort of love did he dare talk to him about? What love was he trying to mollify him, overpower him, debase him with?

Father Elías folded his hands, as though preparing to pray. And he began to talk very quietly, while Fernando listened to him, pale and trembling:

"Captain, Sir: When you were a child you slept in my arms many times while I told you how Baby Jesus, in the arms of Saint Anthony, played with the light of the stars. When your mother died, I attended to her until the last minute, and even closed her eyes with my fingers, and I blessed the ground where she rests. Likewise, I attended to your poor sister and gave your unfortunate father a Christian burial. Do I have the right to a little consideration, affection, gratitude for all this?"

Fernando's voice trembled, nearly sobbing:

"What do you want? What are you suggesting? Speak up, tell me."

Father Elías continued:

"These hands that closed your mother's eyes, have come to open the eyes of her son. You are here, sir, like Lazarus in his grave. I am here to awaken you in the name of God. Untie your bonds! Come out of that burial chamber of darkness and death! Let us go out to the light and to life, Captain!"

"And my justice, the justice I swore I would carry out for my poor dead ones, for my wounded country?"

"In your case, that justice is called revenge, sir."

"Whatever its name is, I have to do it!"

"No! Leave it in the hands of God! Because what we men take for Justice, if it were truly Justice, why did God call all those millions of people 'blessed' who are so unfortunate, those beings in the world who tremble with hunger and thirst for Justice?"

There was a long silence while Fernando, his head held between his hands, seemed to meditate bitterly. Until Father Elías spoke again:

"You were always a good Christian and a great patriot. Unfortunately, you're not that anymore. Because living the way you do, devoting your soul and your life to vengeance, no matter how noble, how lofty, how holy the reasons are, is the same as raising up the cross again of the One who forgave his executioners in Golgotha. And to head a party of rebels who are sowing terror and chaos, instead of embracing law and peace, is to foment crime!"

Robles sprang up, livid, raging:

"Watch what you say! You're not talking to sacristans or cloister sisters here! A little more of that, and I'll throw you out like a piece of slag!"

But at that same instant, several shots rang out, and instead of answering, Father Elías made the sign of the cross. Immediately afterward, as though obeying a command, several men appeared. Alarmed, Fernando asked:

"What was that?"

The men smiled, and one of them explained the matter. Nothing serious, Captain. Pablo ordered them to shoot the Japanese prisoner. Why treat his wounds? Why give him anything to eat? They needed the medicine and rice more than anyone...

"And who is Pablo to give orders that contradict mine?" Robles shouted wildly. "Have you gone mad all of a sudden? Tell Pablo to answer to me for the life of that Japanese!"

He turned back to the priest:

"Come looking for me tomorrow. Let me think! Give me time to talk with God and with my soul tonight. For me, you're like temptation, self-denial, the collapse of a very lofty idea and a holy belief. Stay over there, with those men, or wherever you can... And don't forget to pray, Father Elías! Pray for the souls of my loved ones, pray for my soul"

Several days afterward, with great strides, as though anxious to leave that place forever, without looking back even once to see what they were leaving behind, they hurriedly went down, through the intricate labyrinths of the mountain, covered in greenery, splashed with colorful wildflowers. And inside the fighter's chest, his poor heart of a poet became inflamed under this immense kiss of wild springtime. Lively colors and ripe aromas spoke to him powerfully, with new words. Why kill? Why die? They had sisters who were much more beautiful than themselves, except that they were called women. And a perfume more intense than that which all the fields and all the altars could emanate. And this perfume was called love.

Life...! Love...! He remembered the Japanese that his men had shot. And the poor lieutenant who fell beside him at the battlefront of Bataan. They both cherished the hope, the sweetest fantasy of men, of not losing their lives. They both dreamed of nests cooing with the laughter of children and the voices of women. They both risked their lives while clinging to the desire to live. They both went into the night with the spark of excitement before their eyes and a garland of hope in their hands.

Why couldn't he, Fernando, now feel or think like that pair of wretched men, so enamored with love and life? There was a time when he had felt that way, and even more deeply still, when everything seemed beautiful, when his heart was very good. That time flashed and went out like a bolt of lightning. Who had girded his eyes with such a black blindfold? Who had snuffed out the light of his pathway? Who had turned his heart?

It was not pain. Pain purifies the soul and makes men better than they are. Pain, be it a wound of the flesh, a laceration of the soul, lifts us to heaven and brings us close to God. And now Fernando barely thought about God. Nor did he think about himself, for he did not recognize himself when he looked into the mirror of life.

Suddenly he held onto Father Elías:

"Do you think I've changed?"

The priest looked at him with pity:

"Yes, sir. When you were up there, at the head of that mob of men. Now he was turning back into what he always was, a gentleman. He had gotten rid of that dirty laundry, that horrible past..."

"You don't have the smell of blood now, Captain, sir. You don't have the look of men who seem to have death lurking in their eyes..."

They finally reached the plain, and the marsh suddenly appeared where several carabao were sloshing and lowing contentedly. Further on, the green silk canopy of the rustling banana plantations rose up. Scattered flocks of white goats and black goats dipped into the leafy, fragrant herbs. Disturbed and disruptive hens quickly crossed the path to escape the harassment of the amorous rooster. The barking of dogs and pounding of a mortar could be heard over the wooden "lusong"[87] where golden palay[88] was ground to powder, and in its place the rosy nacre of new rice appeared. And finally, as they went through the foliage, the first village stood out, a quiet life, peaceful, orderly people.

Fernando stopped before the panorama unveiled before him: the good earth and the burning sun. For some time he had been listening distractedly to the news that Father Elías had been telling him about the war. None of that seemed to matter to him. Italy destroyed; Germany crushed; so, what? The entire world could go plummeting down! Nothing mattered to him anymore. He was still lost in his reverie of grief. Why wake up?

But this village, these people, this gentle existence that he had abandoned forever and that now, caressing and sweet like a new Samaritan, came out to meet him, seemed to instill him with new blood and sweep away from his mind the last disagreeable thoughts. To live, yes, live, even if it was with suffering! And to love, to go on loving until the end of his life!

From deep in his breast, from the bottom of his heart there rose up, like a sudden sobbing, the memory of the beloved woman. He was going to her, he was going back to her, without realizing that he was inspired by love and life. What should he go back for, and why go back at all, if it were not for her alone? That brown farmhouse, that emerald field, those colorful flowers...

"Marta, my Marta, flower of the fields...!"

His heart called out to her, like a newly awakened child calls out for its mother, like a wounded bird returning to its nest calls out for its mate, like a man lost at night calls out to the heavens.

"Marta, my Marta, flower of the fields...!"

Thank you, Father Elías, thank you. He was turning again into what he always was. He was beginning to recognize himself, and once again he found that he was the same man that he had tried in vain to find only a short while before. He no longer had the smell of blood, but of flowers. And instead of the dirty jacket the priest had spoken of, he was walking sheathed in the dazzling breeze of the gold and diamond scales of divine hope.

But life is not a fairy tale that always ends happily. Grief pursued him, it did not want to leave him, it went before him like his shadow under the sun, across life, along the road. And so it was, because when he reached the city days later, and went searching for his sweetheart, hungry and thirsty for love, he did not find her. Don Ramon, holding him in a tight embrace, told him sadly:

"Her parents insisted on going out to the provinces, and I doubt that they're in town. They must have gone into the hills. Didn't you just get back from there...?"

To return, giving up the horror of his past, prepared to never leave her again, certain that he would find her waiting for him, desperate with love among her roses, and not find her! To have shirked his duty and renounced vengeance with the unconfessed and secret sentiment he had placed in her, for this enormous disappointment. Why had they left each other forever? Why had they parted...? Why, if they never...?

He thought that his first duty was to sacrifice his heart for his country. Sacrifice it then before the bloody drama in which the Filipinos perished. If the night when he believed for the last time that his heart did not have the courage to shout, to call out to her, so that he would not lose his life at the foot of her window, what was the point of suffering, sighing, and collapsing in tears?

When she offered the honey on her lips to him, he wanted to be a man of steel. He fled from the paradise that the window offered to him. And the illusion punished him mercilessly.`

He deserved it. Let his romantic heart go on crying in vain. No one can mock love. Because love, more than anyone, knows how to avenge itself, knows how to make one suffer, knows how to kill!

V

One day, after many sad days had gone by, the eagles from America veiled the splendor of the sun with their wings. The Philippine sky was their friend, and the clouds of nacre and silver lost their petals like enormous lilies in their wake. Cannons thundered, fire and iron fell from on high, and thick columns of smoke crowned with offshoots of purple and gold arose into space from the wounded earth. Hail America: good, great and powerful!

The grandiloquent Japanese defense consisted of concealing their troops, using trees and shrubs, and burying themselves in bomb shelters with the lizards and rats. If anyone wanted to die, let the Filipinos die, the hundreds, the thousands of Filipinos who sprang up from everywhere, looking up, to bless with closed lips, and with trembling hearts to kiss the wings of America.

In the meanwhile, where were the birds of fire? In what bowels of what abyss had the enormous cynicism, audacity and lies of this terrified Japan sought shelter? The night passed by, treachery and crime gave way. This was America, Mr. Japan. The eagles were returning to their nest.

The black curtain was about to fall over the horrifying three-year tragedy. But first, the yellow man of this farce was throwing his

Japanese mask of a heroic Samurai on the ground, appearing in his true form, revealing his ugly head of a cynical and cowardly assassin. Oh, the hideous idol of war, the false god that was tumbling down from his pedestal of clay to turn to dust, ash, smoke...!

"Mio carissimo dottore!"

"Distinguished professor!"

The shadows of Mussolini and Hitler made up one lone shadow on the sidewalk of the plaza of Santa Cruz. Anselmi and Von Kauffman shook hands. The Italian's hand, smooth, delicate and sparkling with precious gems; the German's, dark, hairy, rough, strong as a claw...

"How is life, professor?"

"Oh, la vita, misera, porca vitae! He hadn't even reached a million with his deposits in the banks, killing himself the way he was doing in the business of buying a jewel for a thousand pesos, just to sell it five months later for twenty or thirty thousand! And he, a genius, a musical prince, was sacrificing Art for this! Misera vita. Porca misery! Japanese pigs...!"

Japanese pigs? Even greater swine than the Fascist had imagined. They turned out to be the complete and total negation of all lawfulness, all decency and all civilization. They were showing their hand in this war of the Pacific in an indecent, dishonorable way. They were never fighting just against England and the United States. Their aim was to wipe out the entire white race...

"They've been using us, they've taken advantage of our victories to carry out their horrible work."

On the sidewalk where they were talking, men, women and children were lying face up in the sun, covered with rags and flies, dying of hunger.

Above them, indifferently tripping over their painful agony, swarmed a rabble of sellers and buyers of all sorts of merchandise, their handbags and wallets bulging with money.

From time to time a banknote worth ten, twenty or fifty centavos fluttered down on the dying. The poor things! Why should they eat! Why didn't they just starve to death! And a sweet potato the size of a man's finger cost ten or fifteen pesos at the market.

"Let's get out of here, doctor. Let me buy you a beer. These people, tutta these people, the ones on their backs and the ones standing up, they all smell so bad! Porca misery! What a bunch of riff-raff!"

They went into a canteen of English Indians along the Escolta. Huge lithographs hanging from the walls displayed replicas of two great monstrosities, Ba Maw[89] and Chandra Bose.[90] The premises were stuffed full of people drinking and eating lavishly. Several young ladies lured people in, and waited on tables, scandalously dressed and painted up. And standing out prominently, above and among them all, an enormous Japanese flag stretching grandly, like the bed sheet of a prostitute who had just given birth, stained in blood.

"Hello, Sili, bring us some beer."

It was Anselmi talking. And in hushed tones to the German:

"This girl, the one you see here, is from a very distinguished family. Except that she's a zebra. Before, she used to give it to the Spaniards and the Americans, and now she gives it to the Hindus and the Japanese…"

The German shrugged:

"You think she's the only one? Multiply her by a thousand!"

"The beauty of it will be afterward, when the Americans come back, if they're even able to come back. All these girls will be like the stars and stripes. Hello Joe, over here; hello Joe, over there; hello Joe, everywhere!"

"That story, for sure!"

"Poor woman, poor country, poor... Porca squalor!"

At that instant the entire building shook and a tremendous explosion, followed by others farther away, raised torrents of fire and rocks all along the Escolta. Bridges and buildings began to fly apart, and the people, in mortal panic, started running wildly from one side to another, desperately, not knowing where to go, covered with dust, with smoke, and with shrapnel...

"This looks like the end, doctore...!"

They tried to escape, in vain; the street outside was much more dangerous...

"Yes, it looks like these brutes are up to their old tricks... That carabao Yamashita[91] woke up today with an itch to start goring people..."

But Anselmi was not listening now. Pale and trembling, he prayed with clenched teeth and a choked voice:

"Santa Madona...! Santa Mare de Dio...! Blessed Santo Pancracio...!"

Enormous explosions followed, along with the sounds of bullets and great cries of fear, of pain, for help. The rumbling was becoming unbearable. Suddenly a group of Japanese soldiers invaded the canteen; sabers and bayonets were stained with blood...

"Hey...! I be Italian...! Fascist...! Nephew of the great Mussolini...!"

He fell, crying out, with a bayonet stuck in his belly. At the same time, Von Kauffman fell beside him, his skull split open by the blade of a saber. Soon afterward, the canteen was turned into a huge pile of raped women and slaughtered men.

One month earlier the Japanese had left the Robles house. Sacked and torn apart, they deigned to return it to its owners. Fernando and Don Ramon went back to it, and they met there on that unforgettable morning.

The Captain was carrying, like a relic on his chest, upon his tormented heart, the letter that he had recently received from Marta. He had read it so many times that he could repeat it from memory... "Be careful, protect yourself, live! It is only a matter of days, perhaps only hours, when we'll be together again. And then nothing will be able to separate us, will it...?"

Nothing! Only death. And that wouldn't come. He had challenged it many times, and it had always fled. It was afraid of him, it shrank from him, it gave him clear passage. He could walk down the open road with his beloved virgin, a sweet burden of love in his arms, toward the luminous morning, to where the larks sang, toward the leafless roses of the new dawn.

Above the nearby roar of the explosions and the artillery fire, louder than the voice of his heart speaking to him of his beloved lady, came the shouts of Don Ramon who was stumbling toward him with outstretched arms like a Christ who had just come off the cross and was about to fall...

"Fernando...! Fernando...! They're here now...! They're very close now, fighting, advancing...!"

"Who?"

"The Americans, my boy!"

He ran to the balcony, opened it wide, looked outside. The street was swarming with Japanese troops in fervent retreat. And from the entire Ermita and all the districts there arose enormous pyramids of fire coming from the buildings and the blocks of dynamited, burning houses. All along every street, machine guns were firing at residents who were anxiously trying to get to safety. And before he closed the balcony, Fernando was horrified to see how a poor woman fell to her knees before a Japanese soldier, holding up the little body of her son, begging for mercy. The Japanese snatched away the child, stabbing it with his bayonet, and threw it, dead, against the stones, and then shot the poor thing.

A neighbor ran up, bringing terrifying news. They had to run away, get to safety, no matter how, and right now. The Japanese had no respect for anything. He had even seen how they were firing on the consulates, and how foreigners were falling under the crashing flight of their flags, shot up, vilified, ridiculed. There were no longer any Germans, Italians, French, Spaniards, Russians, Swiss. Now there were only whites, naïve, disarmed whites. And instead of confronting the American tanks that were laying into them, spitting out fire, they were using their last efforts to burn, murder, destroy, in defense of their emperor, of their flag, and of the Bushido, the sadly notorious and famous code of their honor.

"Hurry up, for God's sake...! Move...! You have to get away...!"

Hand grenades, flung against the house, began to fall from trees in the garden. Fernando, holding onto Ramon, began pulling him to the great staircase...

"Let's go, uncle."

But the old man resisted:

"To where? And what for? If we have to die, let's die. Death is everywhere..."

Fernando insisted, shouting nervously:

"No, no! We have to see if we can get away! Right now, more than ever, I need life, more than ever, my Marta...!

He took him by force, almost dragging him, while the old man fell to his knees and finally let himself be carried like a dry leaf through the wind. The bullets whistled as they came in everywhere. One of them brought down Fernando.

Don Ramon felt him fall, and then saw him bloodied and broken on the ground, before the neighbor put him on his shoulders and carried him like a child, fleeing through the garden under the shelter of the orchard and the walls until they reached the boulevard. There they could hide among the rocks.

"Do you think my nephew is dead?"

"And do you think that if he was alive, we would have left him? Look over there, at your house! A huge inferno!"

Shaken with sobbing, the old man rested against the rock so that he would not fall. Poor Fernando! Poor Ermita! Poor Philippines! He wept freely, and because he was thirsty, with a painful, burning thirst, he quenched it with his great tears.

Was it hours? Was it days? How much time went by in the existence of Don Ramon Robles, nestled in his stone hiding place, his back turned to the devastated town, facing the sea illuminated by the reflection of the final flames? He had slept or he had fallen into a faint. When he woke up he was alone. His companion had left. It was night, but it was also life.

"Thank you, my Lord!"

He could barely keep his memories straight; he could barely give an exact account of what had happened on this night. A sharp, persistent pain was pounding at his temples, and while he was trying to keep his eyelids open, they closed, falling heavily on his sore eyes like two lead plates.

"Thank you, my Lord!"

Not for having saved him, an old wreck. For having saved the Philippines, Lord!

He was thirsty, horribly thirsty, ravenously thirsty. He tried to stand up, to walk, but he was unable. He fainted again. He closed his eyes...

And suddenly all of space and the entire sea became bright. A ship appeared upon the waters. And from the ship came a cry in Spanish...

Christopher Columbus, glorious Admiral! Great and divine the day when, on the bridge of the "Santa Maria," he shouted "land" before the vision of America. Kneeling before it, he saw it appear beautiful and virginal, like an aurora of sweet fire fallen upon the waves by the hand of God. Then he kissed its bare flesh, illuminated by the flash of its precious stones. And between the eagle wings of its crown he attached the cross of his magnificent banner. And overwhelmed by its extraordinary enchantment, he surrendered his sword at its naked feet. Immortal, great deed, Admiral! For now his romantic heart sensed that throughout life and history, the wonderful vision that he adored, trembling with hope, would be redemption for those peoples who lacked liberty, a firm support for fallen humanity, bread and wine of love for those who have hunger and thirst for justice, a bed of feathers and flowers for the wounded world...

THE END
New Manila
Quezon City, 1945

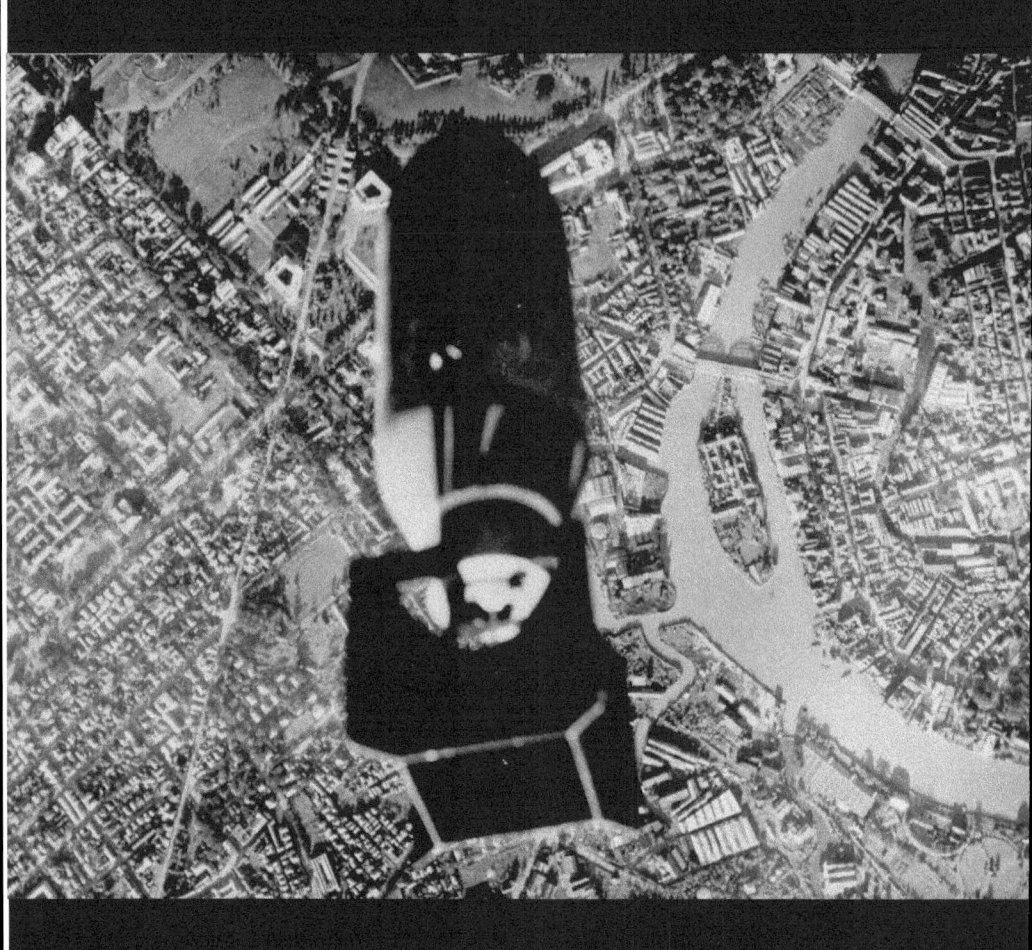

Bomb bay camera in a TBF-1 Avenger from USS Essex captures the moment of bomb release over the Pasig River in downtown Manila, Luzon, Philippines, 14 Nov 1944
Source: United States Navy National Museum of Naval Aviation
Retrieved from: https://ww2db.com/image.php?image_id=24254

Notes

[1] Izanagi and Izanami: the central deities of the Shinto religion who are believed to have created the islands of Japan.
[2] Amaterasu: the sun goddess of the Shinto religion.
[3] Susanoo: the storm god of Japanese mythology; he is the younger brother of the sun goddess Amaterasu.
[4] Jimmu-tennō: According to legend, the first Emperor of Japan (660 B.C.E- 585 B.C.E.) and a descendant of the sun goddess Amaterasu.
[5] Nikko: a city located in Tochigi Prefecture, Japan.
[6] Nara: city in south-central Honshu, Japan. Deer from this area were once considered sacred.
[7] Kamakura: a seaside Japanese city south of Tokyo in Japan.
[8] Daibutsu: a Japanese term used for large statues of Buddha.
[9] Nipponese: American English term for Japanese person or language.
[10] Ermita: a district in Manila.
[11] Salgari: Emilio Salgari (1862–1911), Italian writer of adventure stories and novels.
[12] Legazpi: Miguel López de Legazpi (c. 1510-1572), Spanish explorer and first governor of the Philippines.
[13] Urdaneta: Andrés de Urdaneta (1498-1568), Spanish navigator and Augustinian friar who discovered a path across the Pacific from the Philippines o Acapulco that was used by the Manila galleons.
[14] Visayas: Visayas is one of the three main island groups of the Philippines, along with Luzón and Mindanao.
[15] Garibaldi: Giuseppe Garibaldi (1807-1882), Italian patriot and soldier who helped the Italian unification under the royal house of Savoy.
[16] Mussolini: Benito Amilcare Andrea Mussolini (1883-1945), Fascist dictator of Italy during World War II; also known as Il Duce ("The Leader").

[17] Verdi: Giuseppe Fortunino Francesco Verdi (1813-1901), leading Italian composer of opera.
[18] Caruso: Enrico Caruso (1873-1921), noted Italian operatic tenor.
[19] Tita Rufo: (1877-1953), Italian operatic baritone.
[20] Toselli: Enrico Toselli (1883-1926), Italian pianist and composer.
[21] Radamés: captain of the guard in Verdi's opera, *Aida*.
[22] Bocato di cardinali: boccato di cardinale - "an exquisite dish."
[23] Il Duce: See "Mussolini."
[24] Axis: The major Axis Powers in World War II were Germany, Italy, and Japan.
[25] Vinta boat: a traditional boat from the Philippine island of Mindanao.
[26] Balitao: a Philippine peasant dance.
[27] Buddha: Siddhārtha Gautama (c. 5th to 4th century BCE), founder of Buddhism.
[28] Shōgun: in Japanese history, a military ruler.
[29] Samurai: member of the Japanese warrior caste.
[30] Daimyo: Japanese feudal lord.
[31] Musme: a Japanese maiden.
[32] Guatama: Siddhartha Gautama (c. 5th to 4th century BCE), Indian spiritual teacher known as the Buddha.
[33] Yoshiwara: a famous red-light district in Tokyo, Japan.
[34] Mikado: the Emperor of Japan.
[35] Othello: Jealous lover in the play by William Shakespeare *The Tragedy of Othello, the Moor of Venice*.
[36] Ohayo: Japanese greeting for "Good morning."
[37] Yeyasu: Tokugawa Ieyasu (1543-1616), the founder and first shōgun of the Tokugawa shogunate of Japan.
[38] Shamisen: a lute-like three-stringed traditional Japanese musical instrument; it is played with a plectrum called a bachi.

[39] Kuruma: "car" in Japanese.
[40] Kalipulako: Lapu-Lapu (c. 1490-1542), a ruler of Mactan in the Visayas; defeated and killed the Portuguese explorer Ferdinand Magellan in 1521.
[41] Lakandula: king of the pre-colonial Philippine Kingdom of Tondo when the Spaniards first conquered the lands of the Pasig River delta in the 1570s.
[42] Sikatuna: chief on the island of Bohol; made a blood compact and alliance with the Spanish explorer Miguel López de Legazpi in 1565.
[43] Solimán: Rajah Sulayman (1558-1575), Muslim ruler of the Kingdom of Maynila; fought the Spanish conquerors.
[44] "The poet fell, singing before his death": poem by José Rizal (1861-1896).
[45] Bonifacio: Andrés Bonifacio y de Castro (1863-1897), Filipino revolutionary leader and the president of the Tagalog Republic.
[46] Mabini: Apolinario Mabini y Maranan (1864-1903), a Filipino revolutionary leader and the first Prime Minister of the First Philippine Republic (1899); his work "El Verdadero Decálogo" expressed the ideals he believed the Philippine Revolution should have.
[47] Luna: Antonio Luna de San Pedro y Novicio Ancheta (1866-1899) Filipino army general who fought in the Philippine-American War (1899-1902).
[48] Hitler: Adolf Hitler (1889-1945), infamous leader of the Nazi Party in Germany, became chancellor of Germany in 1933 and then Führer in 1934.
[49] Deutschland über alles: "Germany above all;" the national anthem of Germany since 1922, also identified with the Nazi regime in World War II.
[50] Harakiri: also known as *seppuku*, it is ritual suicide by disembowelment originally practiced by the samurai but was later practiced by other Japanese people to restore honor.
[51] Rigoletto: an opera by Giuseppe Verdi (1813-1901).
[52] Cavite: a province in the Philippines located on Luzón island.
[53] Wagner: Wilhelm Richard Wagner (1813-1883), a German composer, theatre director, and conductor who is chiefly known for his operas.

[54] Goethe: Johann Wolfgang von Goethe (1749-1832), German poet, playwright, novelist.
[55] Heine: Christian Johann Heinrich Heine (1797-1856), German poet.
[56] Kurumeros: People who pull "rickshaws" in Japan.
[57] Parsifal: an opera by German composer Richard Wagner.
[58] Quijote: *El ingenioso hidalgo don Quijote de la Mancha*, novel by Miguel de Cervantes.
[59] Caesar: 'Veni, vidi, vici.': Latin phrase attributed to Julius Caesar, meaning "I came; I saw; I conquered."
[60] Gayda: Virginio Gayda (1885-1944), prominent Italian Fascist and journalist.
[61] Brunetti: Angelo Brunetti (1800—1849), Italian patriot.
[62] Koto: Japanese board zither.
[63] Geisha: in Japan, a woman trained in the arts of music, dance and entertaining.
[64] Solomon: According to biblical accounts, king of the United Kingdom of Israel who had 700 wives and 300 concubines.
[65] Nietzsche: Friedrich Nietzsche (1844-1900), German philosopher; his book *Also sprach Zarathustra (Thus Spoke Zarathustra)* is a philosophical novel.
[66] Camacho: a figure appearing in Cervantes's novel *El ingenioso hidalgo don Quijote de la Mancha*.
[67] Otto von Bismarck (1815-1898), German statesman responsible for transforming a collection of small German states into the German empire. He was its first chancellor.
[68] Baguio: a mountain town on the Philippines' Luzón island.
[69] Pampango: The language of the inhabitants of Pampanga, in Central Luzón.
[70] Bushido: a collective term for the many codes of conduct and honor that guided the way of life of Japan's warrior class, the Samurai.

[71] Konoe: Prince Fumimaro Konoe (1891-1945), a Japanese politician and Prime Minister.
[72] Tojo: Hideki Tojo (1884-1948), Japanese Army general and Prime Minister of Japan during World War II. When Japan surrendered to the United States, he was arrested and unsuccessfully attempted suicide; later he was hanged as a war criminal.
[73] Nomura and Kurusu: Japanese diplomats, Kichisaburo Nomura (1877-1964) and Saburo Kurusu (1877-1964), had to personally decode the radioed message of Japan's breaking off negotiations with the United States in 1941, while the Japanese government was secretly preparing the attack on Pearl Harbor.
[74] Prometheus: in Greek religion, a Titan and trickster figure who defied the gods by stealing fire and giving it to humanity as civilization. Zeus had him nailed to a rock where each day an eagle would eat his immortal liver.
[75] José Rizal (1861-1896), Filipino patriot, physician, and man of letters; accused of inspiring the Philippine Revolution against Spanish colonial authorities, he was executed by firing squad.
[76] Jacinto: Emilio Jacinto (1875-1899), a Filipino General.
[77] Pilar: Gregorio Hilario del Pilar y Sempio (1875-1899), a Filipino general.
[78] Bataan: a province on the Philippine island of Luzón, infamous during World War II for the Japanese army's cruel forced march of American and Filipino prisoners of war for 60 to 70 miles, which resulted in 5,000-18,000 Filipino deaths and 500-650 American deaths.
[79] Corregidor: Corregidor Island, rocky island located at the entrance of Manila Bay.
[80] Banzai Nippon: Japanese war cry.
[81] Arigato gozaimazu: Japanese expression for "Thank you."
[82] Arayat: Mount Arayat, an inactive volcano on Luzón Island.
[83] Sursum corda: "Lift up your hearts," verse in traditional Eucharistic liturgies.

[84] Shinto: the state religion of Japan until 1945.
[85] Yamada: Kosaku Yamada (1886-1965), a Japanese composer and conductor.
[86] Tagalog: Austronesian language spoken in the Philippines. It is the country's national language and one of the two official ones, along with English.
[87] Lusong: Large wooden mortar for grinding corn.
[88] Palay: Rice that is not yet husked.
[89] Ba Maw: (1893-1977), a Burmese political leader and ally of Japan during World War II.
[90] Chandra Bose: Netaji Subhas Chandra Bose (1897-1945), President of Indian National Congress in 1938 and 1939, and an ally of Germany and Japan in World War II.
[91] Yamashita: Tomoyuki Yamashita (1885—1946), general of the Imperial Japanese Army during World War II.

Destruction in the Walled City (Intramuros district) of old Manila in May 1945, three months after the Battle of Manila.
Source: U.S. Dept. of the Army

ABOUT THE AUTHOR

Jesús Balmori (Manila, Philippines. 1886-1948) was one of the leading writers of the golden age of Philippine literature in Spanish. At age seventeen he published a groundbreaking book in Philippine poetry, *Rimas Malayas* (1904), in which he introduced the aesthetics of *Modernismo* for the first time in the Philippines. In 1926 he received the prestigious Zóbel Prize in the literary genre known as Balagtasan, a form of call-and-response debate conducted in verse. Balmori achieved his greatest recognition as a poet in 1940 with **Mi Casa de Nipa**, a collection of his best poems that won the National Literary Award sponsored by the U.S. Commonwealth Government. In his poetry, Balmori expressed his intention to create a Filipino aesthetic that could transcend *Modernismo* and help establish the identity of Spanish-Philippine literature. He wrote prolifically in many genres, including scathing articles and satirical poems under the pseudonym "Batikuling," criticizing the socio-political establishment and the ruling elite of the times. Balmori was also considered one of the most accomplished novelists of his time. His first two novels, *Bancarrota de almas* (Bankruptcy of Souls, 1911) and *Se deshojó la flor* (Withering Flowers, 1915), attempted to go beyond the romantic novel, developing a social realist narrative with the intention of unveiling Filipino national psychology. His third and last novel, *Los pájaros de fuego* (Birds of Fire, 1945), is a testimonial account of the chaos of war and the destruction of the archipelago during World War II. Written in secret during the years of the Japanese military occupation, it is today considered his most important work. Before his death in 1948, Balmori was able to complete the manuscript of his novel and cede it to the Philippine government for publication. However, *Birds of Fire* was never published and was thought to be lost for over half a century. Its recent rediscovery and publication represents a historic event for the memory of the Filipino people and their literary tradition. This is the first English translation.

ABOUT THE CONTRIBUTORS

Robert S. Rudder holds a doctorate degree in Spanish/ English history from the University of Minnesota (1962-69) with a specialization in Golden Age Spanish Literature. He began translating short stories while teaching Spanish at the University of Minnesota in the 1960s, and later continued his dedication to literary translation during his teaching years at UCLA and other universities in California. He has published twelve books, including a new translation of the picaresque classic novel *Lazarillo de Tormes* (1975), and English translations of such writers as Benito Pérez Galdós, Rosario Castellanos and Cristina Peri Rossi. He has received grants from the Spanish Ministry of Culture for the translation of *Nazarín* by Pérez Galdós (1997); and from the National Endowment for the Arts for *Lo prohibido* by Pérez Galdós (2004) and *Tres y un sueño* by Ana María Matute (2017).

Ignacio López-Calvo is Presidential Chair in the Humanities, Director of the Center for the Humanities, and Professor of Literature at the University of California, Merced. He is the author of more than one hundred articles and book chapters, as well as nine single-authored books and seventeen essay collections. He is the co-executive director of the academic journal *Transmodernity: Journal of Peripheral Cultural Production of the Luso-Hispanic World*, the Palgrave-Macmillan Book Series *"Historical and Cultural Interconnections between Latin America and Asia,"* and the Anthem Press book series *"Anthem Studies in Latin American Literature and Culture Series."* His latest books are *The Mexican Transpacific: Nikkei Writing, Visual Arts, Performance* (forthcoming); *Saudades of Japan and Brazil: Contested Modernities in Lusophone Nikkei Cultural Production* (2019); *Dragons in the Land of the Condor: Tusán Literature and Knowledge in Peru* (2014), and *The Affinity of the Eye: Writing Nikkei in Peru* (2013).

Dulzorada

Ingram Content Group UK Ltd.
Milton Keynes UK
UKHW011814230323
419066UK00005B/386